My Life Beyond
ADHD

A Mayo Clinic patient story
by Hey Gee and Evie

MAYO CLINIC PRESS KIDS

This book is a collaboration between
Fondation Ipsen and Mayo Clinic.

The story has been inspired by
Evie's experience with ADHD.

The words in bold refer to key terms on page 32.

MEDICAL EDITOR

Angela C. Mattke, M.D., Consultant, Community Pediatric & Adolescent Medicine, Mayo Clinic, Rochester, MN; Assistant Professor of Pediatrics, Mayo Clinic College of Medicine and Science, Rochester, MN

SERIES CONCEPTION

Fredric B. Meyer, M.D., Consultant, Department of Neurologic Surgery, Mayo Clinic, Rochester, MN; Executive Dean of Education, Professor of Neurosurgery, Mayo Clinic College of Medicine and Science

James A. Levine, M.D., Ph.D., Professor, President, Fondation Ipsen, Paris, France

Foreword

My name is Evie, and I'm 11 years old. I'm in sixth grade, and I have ADHD. One of the most important things you should know about me is that even though I have ADHD, I can still do everything a typical kid can do ... with my own special twist.

This is my story, but I want you to know there are different kinds of ADHD. Think of how someone gets a cold, but they might have different symptoms than someone else does. That's kind of like how there are different ways to experience ADHD.

My ADHD is mostly about how I pay attention. I always expect myself to do the right thing, and I am capable of doing everything that other kids can do. The trouble is that I get more easily distracted and get a little off track sometimes. When I get distracted, I may lose my train of thought, have trouble finishing a task or struggle to follow directions. Sometimes I even **hyperfocus** on things, which can actually be good if used in the right way. I also have dyslexia, so it's even more important for me to be able to focus on reading and writing.

The great news is that I've gotten the help I need to function without getting as easily distracted. I take medicine that helps "turn down some of the noise," so my brain can think more clearly. I've learned to love being organized, because I can see how it helps me. I also love writing, playing basketball and being with my friends. I've never let my ADHD stop me from accomplishing my goals, and I have many goals!

We are all different in our own ways, but that's what makes us unique. When we are able to show our differences, that can help other people feel more comfortable being themselves.

My parents say I've always been a storyteller. I'm excited to share this story with you.

Evie

"
MY UNIQUE WAY
OF THINKING
"

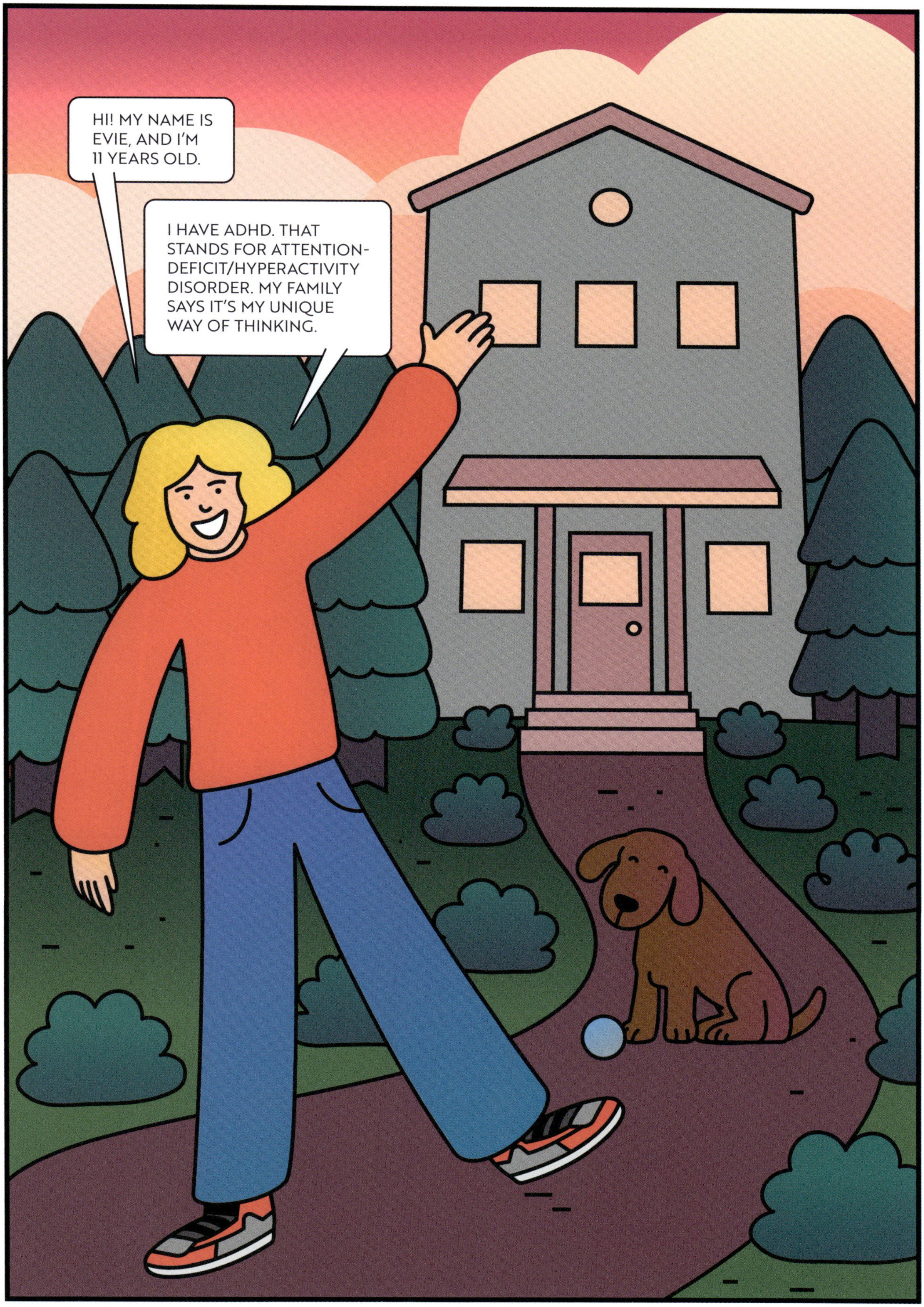
HI! MY NAME IS EVIE, AND I'M 11 YEARS OLD.
I HAVE ADHD. THAT STANDS FOR ATTENTION-DEFICIT/HYPERACTIVITY DISORDER. MY FAMILY SAYS IT'S MY UNIQUE WAY OF THINKING.

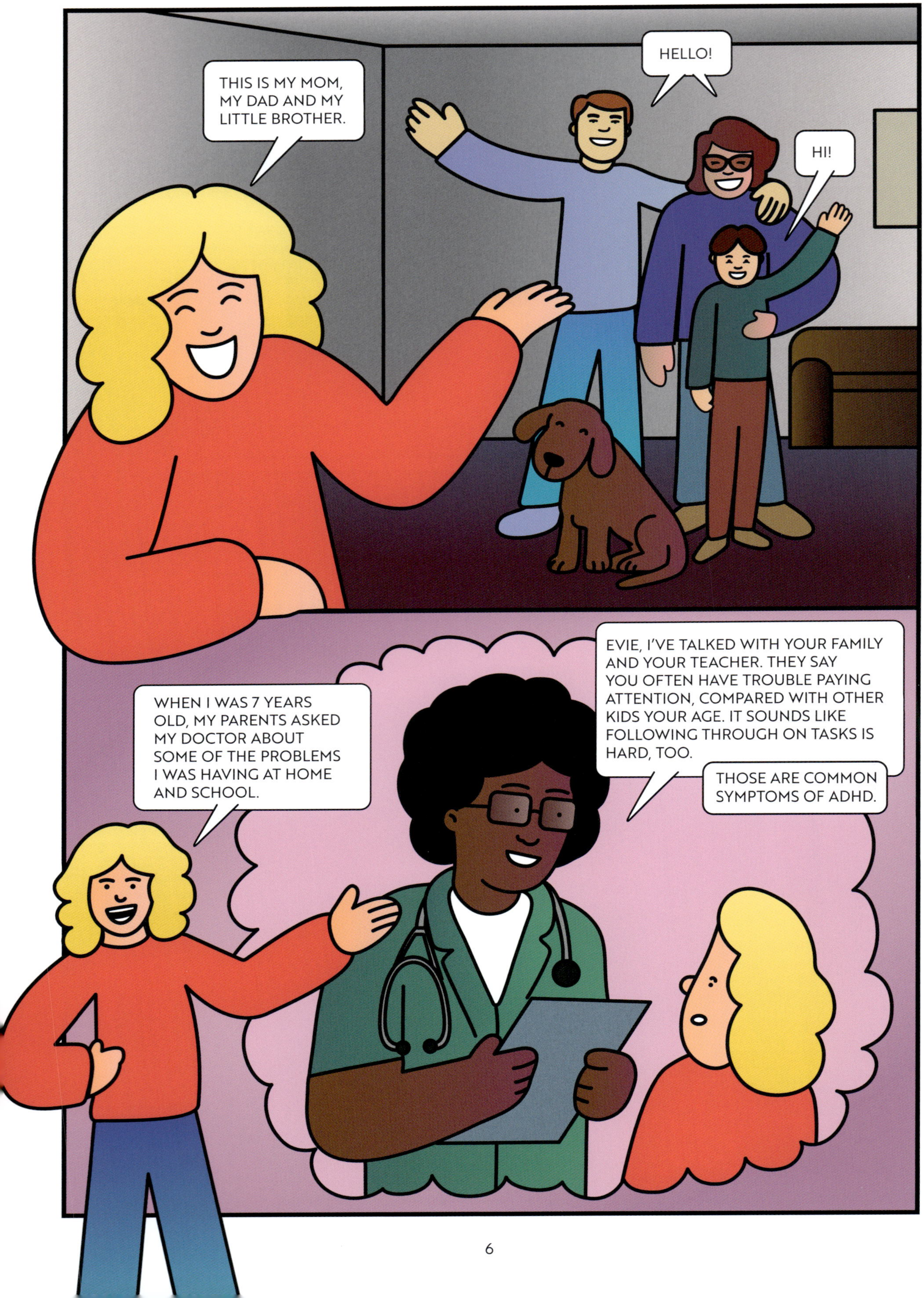
THIS IS MY MOM, MY DAD AND MY LITTLE BROTHER.
HELLO!
HI!
WHEN I WAS 7 YEARS OLD, MY PARENTS ASKED MY DOCTOR ABOUT SOME OF THE PROBLEMS I WAS HAVING AT HOME AND SCHOOL.
EVIE, I'VE TALKED WITH YOUR FAMILY AND YOUR TEACHER. THEY SAY YOU OFTEN HAVE TROUBLE PAYING ATTENTION, COMPARED WITH OTHER KIDS YOUR AGE. IT SOUNDS LIKE FOLLOWING THROUGH ON TASKS IS HARD, TOO.
THOSE ARE COMMON SYMPTOMS OF ADHD.

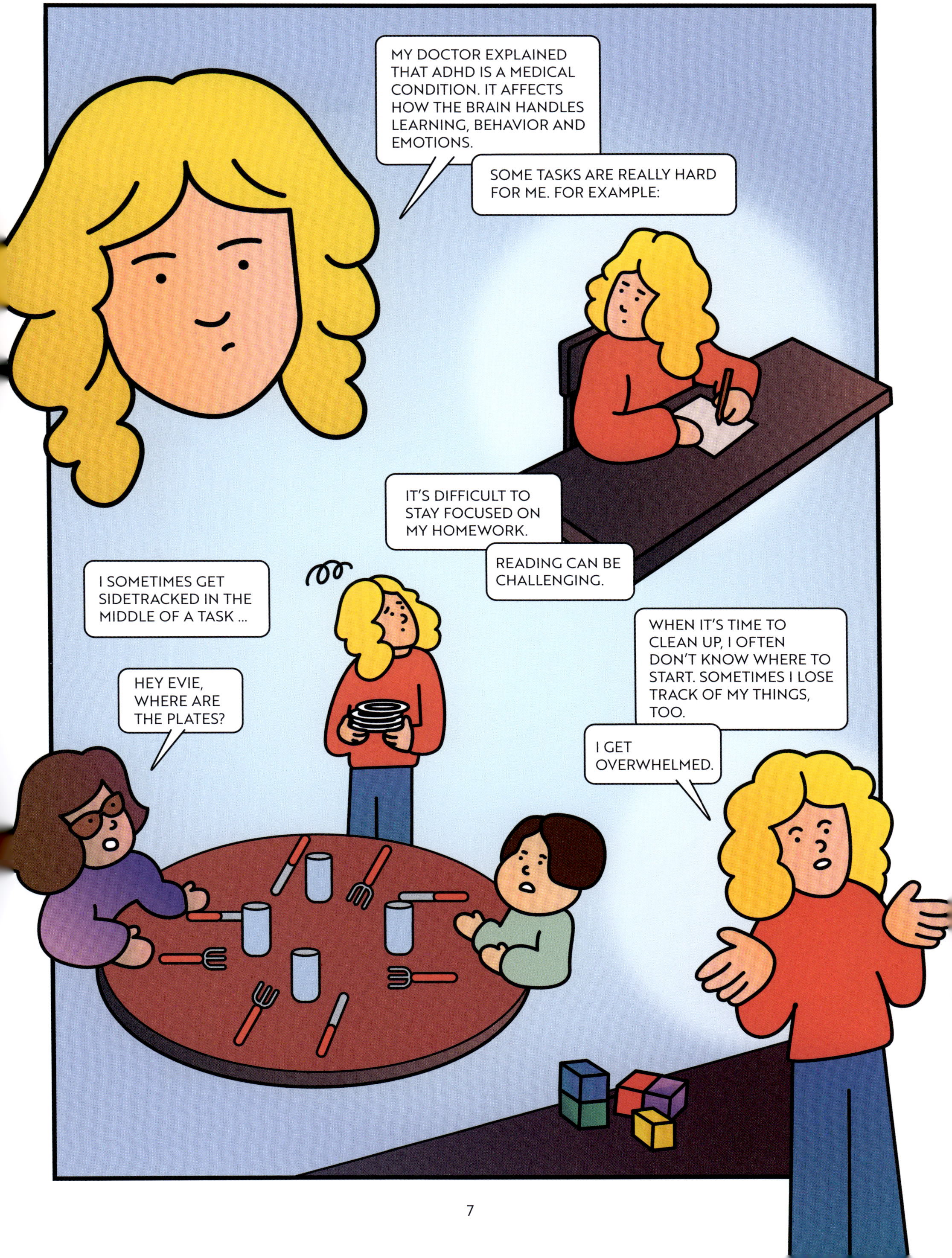
MY DOCTOR EXPLAINED THAT ADHD IS A MEDICAL CONDITION. IT AFFECTS HOW THE BRAIN HANDLES LEARNING, BEHAVIOR AND EMOTIONS.
SOME TASKS ARE REALLY HARD FOR ME. FOR EXAMPLE:
IT'S DIFFICULT TO STAY FOCUSED ON MY HOMEWORK.
READING CAN BE CHALLENGING.
I SOMETIMES GET SIDETRACKED IN THE MIDDLE OF A TASK ...
HEY EVIE, WHERE ARE THE PLATES?
WHEN IT'S TIME TO CLEAN UP, I OFTEN DON'T KNOW WHERE TO START. SOMETIMES I LOSE TRACK OF MY THINGS, TOO.
I GET OVERWHELMED.

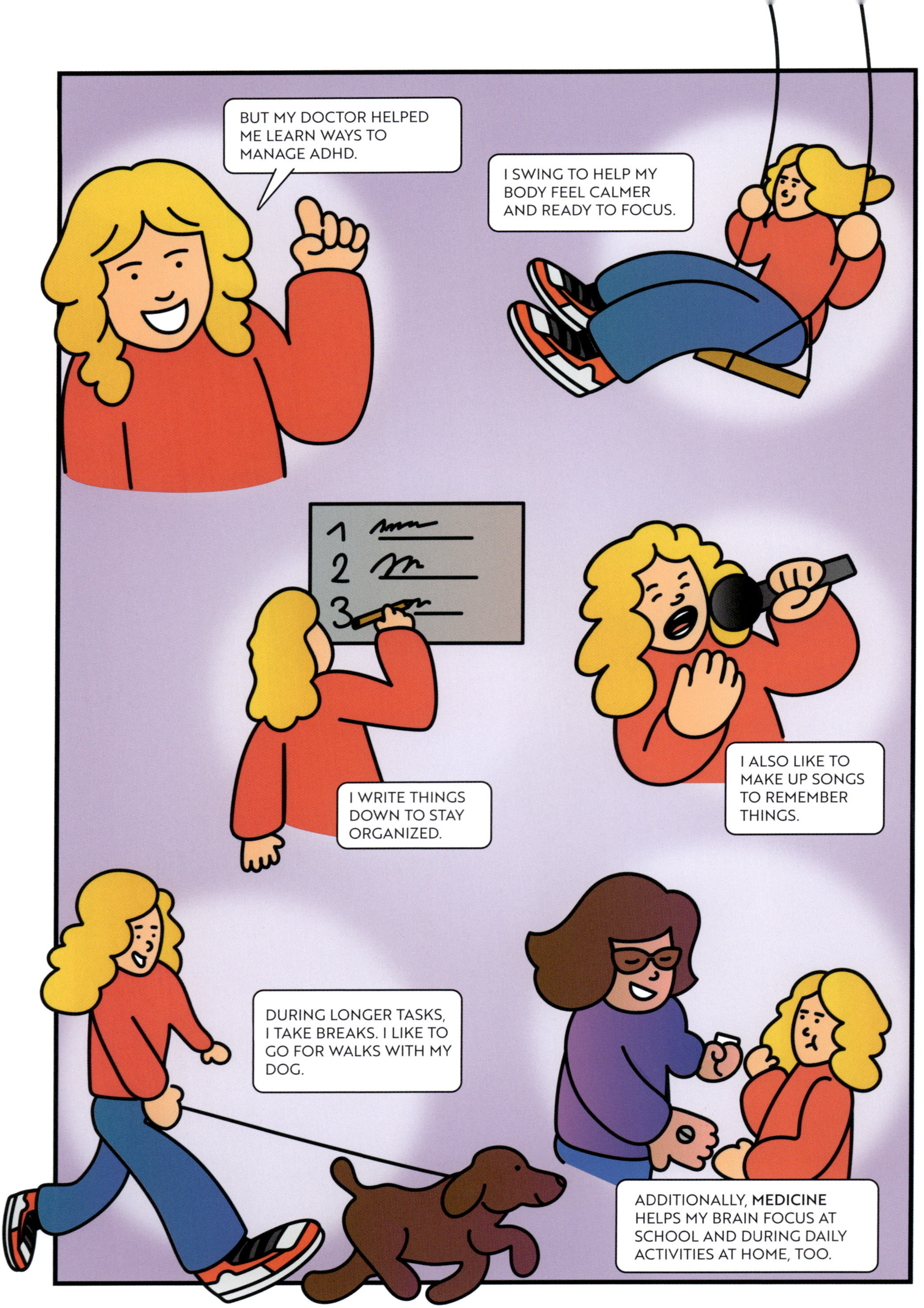
BUT MY DOCTOR HELPED ME LEARN WAYS TO MANAGE ADHD.
I SWING TO HELP MY BODY FEEL CALMER AND READY TO FOCUS.
I WRITE THINGS DOWN TO STAY ORGANIZED.
I ALSO LIKE TO MAKE UP SONGS TO REMEMBER THINGS.
DURING LONGER TASKS, I TAKE BREAKS. I LIKE TO GO FOR WALKS WITH MY DOG.
ADDITIONALLY, **MEDICINE** HELPS MY BRAIN FOCUS AT SCHOOL AND DURING DAILY ACTIVITIES AT HOME, TOO.

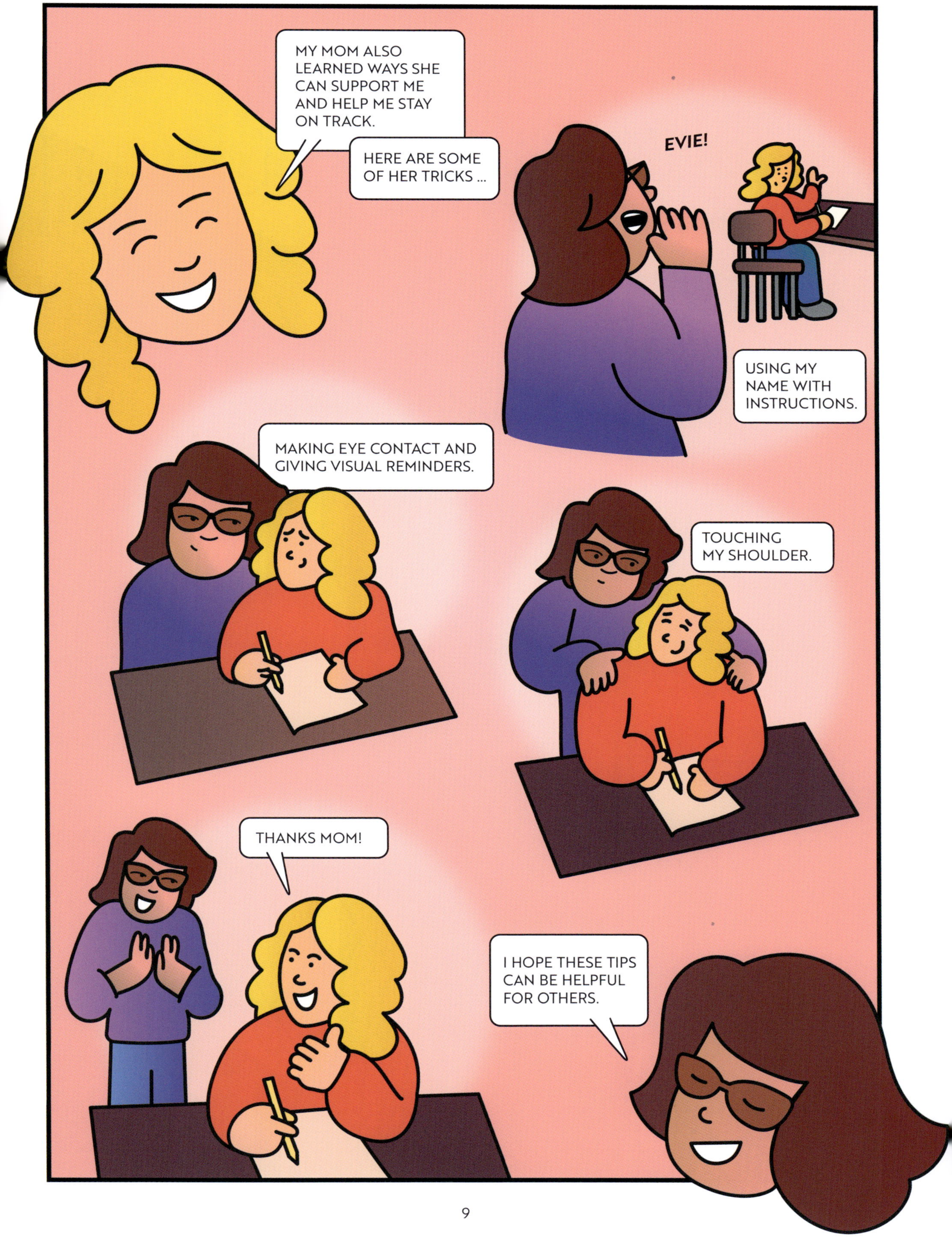
MY MOM ALSO LEARNED WAYS SHE CAN SUPPORT ME AND HELP ME STAY ON TRACK.
HERE ARE SOME OF HER TRICKS ...
EVIE!
USING MY NAME WITH INSTRUCTIONS.
MAKING EYE CONTACT AND GIVING VISUAL REMINDERS.
TOUCHING MY SHOULDER.
THANKS MOM!
I HOPE THESE TIPS CAN BE HELPFUL FOR OTHERS.

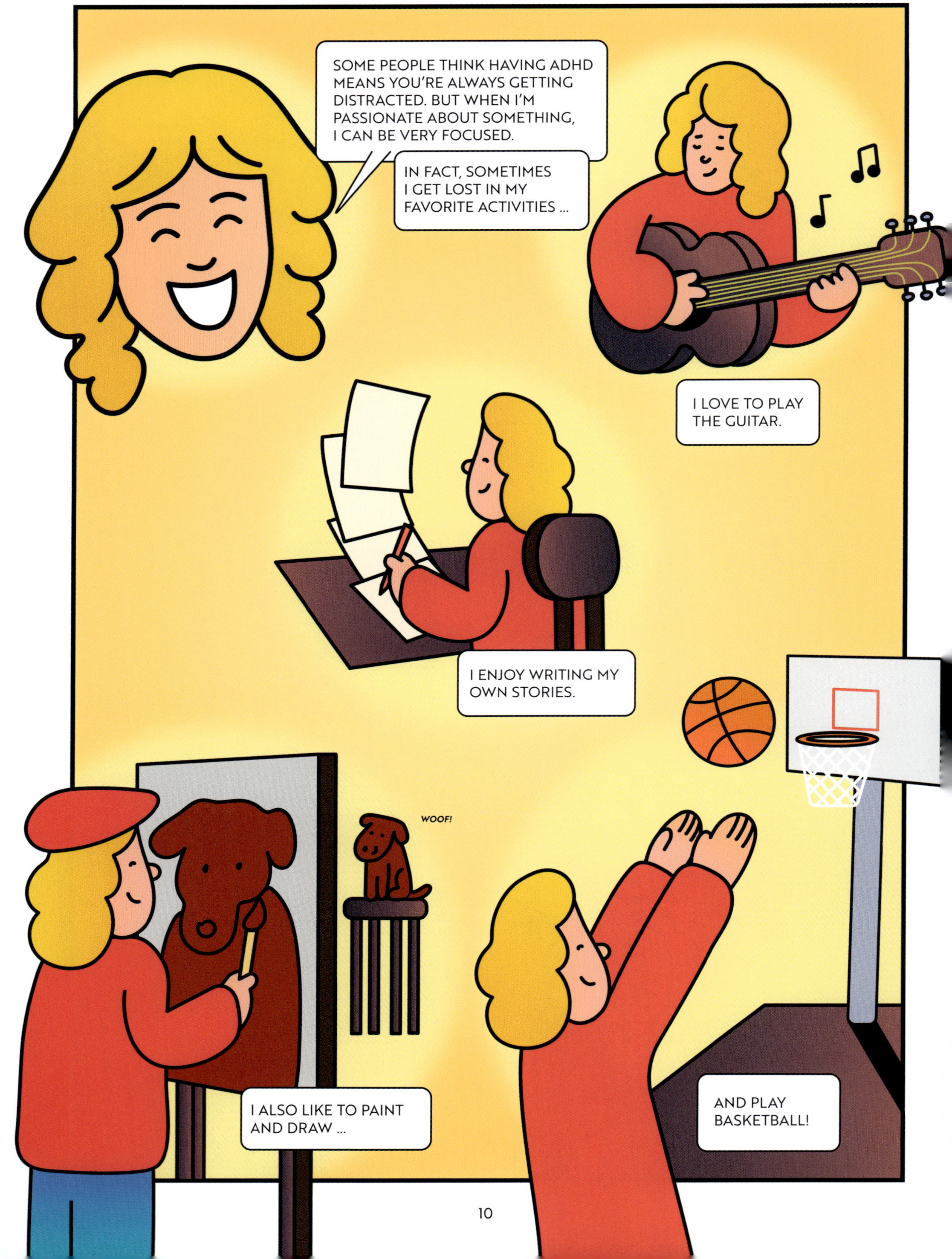
SOME PEOPLE THINK HAVING ADHD MEANS YOU'RE ALWAYS GETTING DISTRACTED. BUT WHEN I'M PASSIONATE ABOUT SOMETHING, I CAN BE VERY FOCUSED.
IN FACT, SOMETIMES I GET LOST IN MY FAVORITE ACTIVITIES ...
I LOVE TO PLAY THE GUITAR.
I ENJOY WRITING MY OWN STORIES.
WOOF!
I ALSO LIKE TO PAINT AND DRAW ...
AND PLAY BASKETBALL!

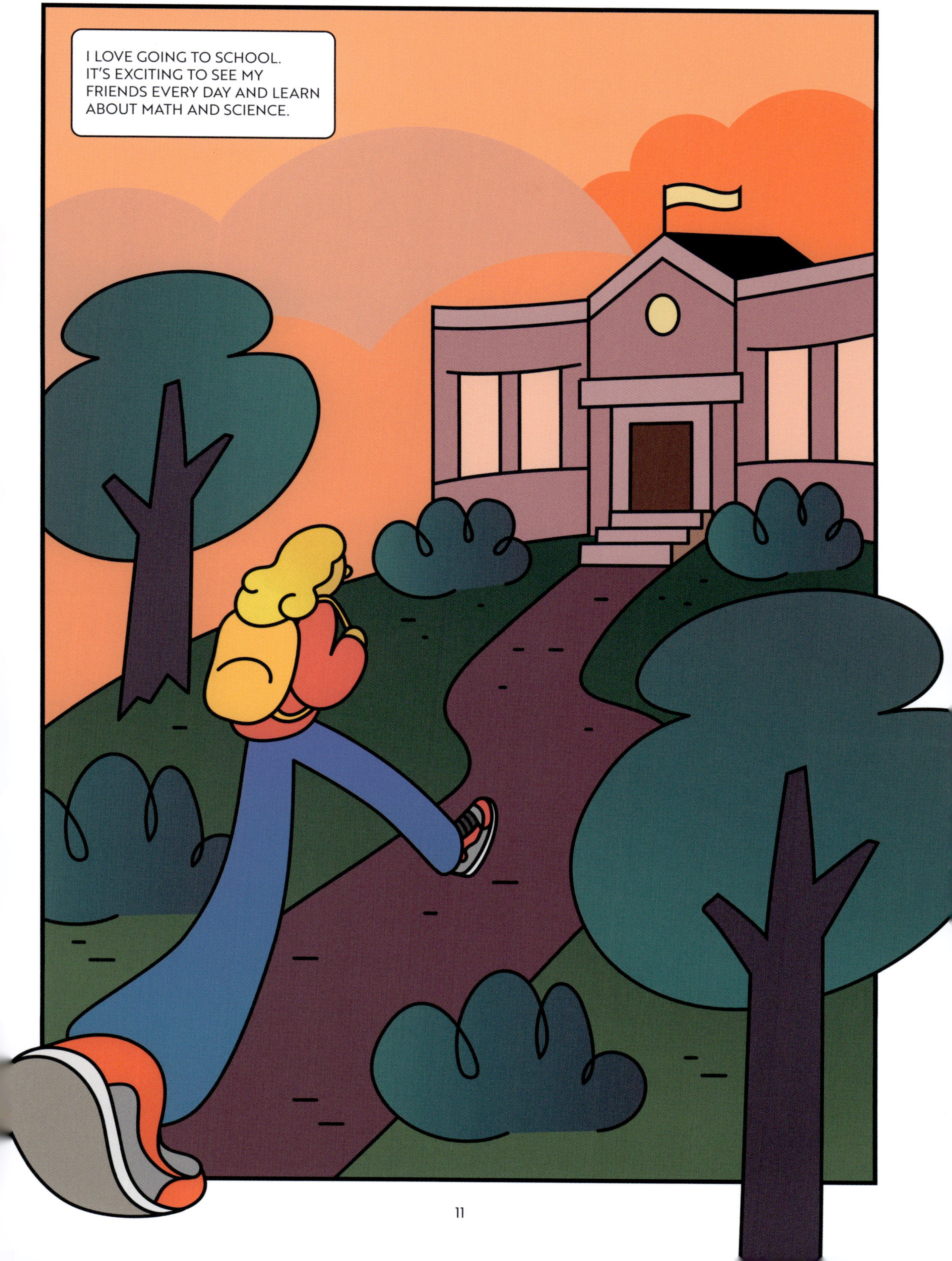
I LOVE GOING TO SCHOOL. IT'S EXCITING TO SEE MY FRIENDS EVERY DAY AND LEARN ABOUT MATH AND SCIENCE.

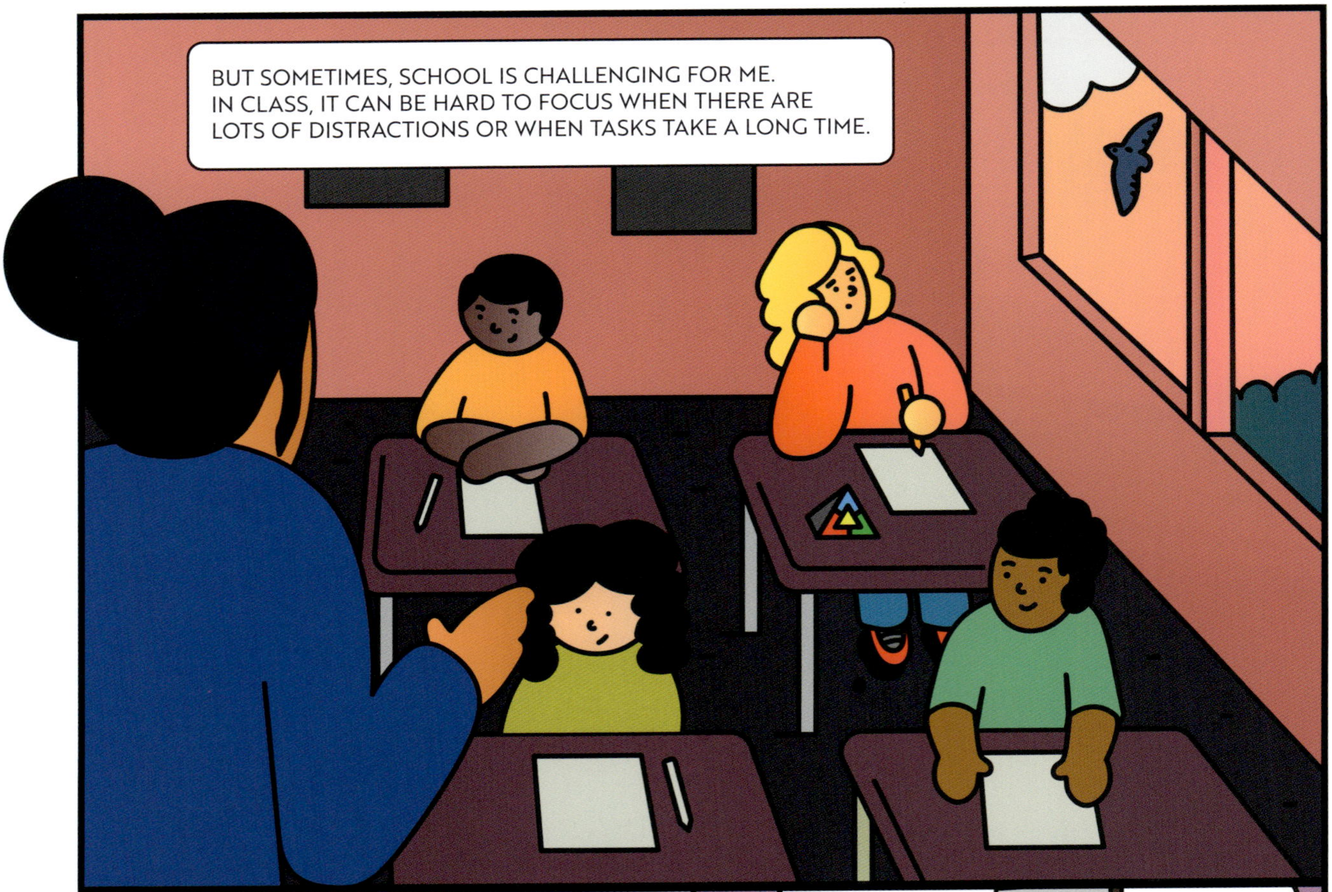
BUT SOMETIMES, SCHOOL IS CHALLENGING FOR ME.
IN CLASS, IT CAN BE HARD TO FOCUS WHEN THERE ARE LOTS OF DISTRACTIONS OR WHEN TASKS TAKE A LONG TIME.

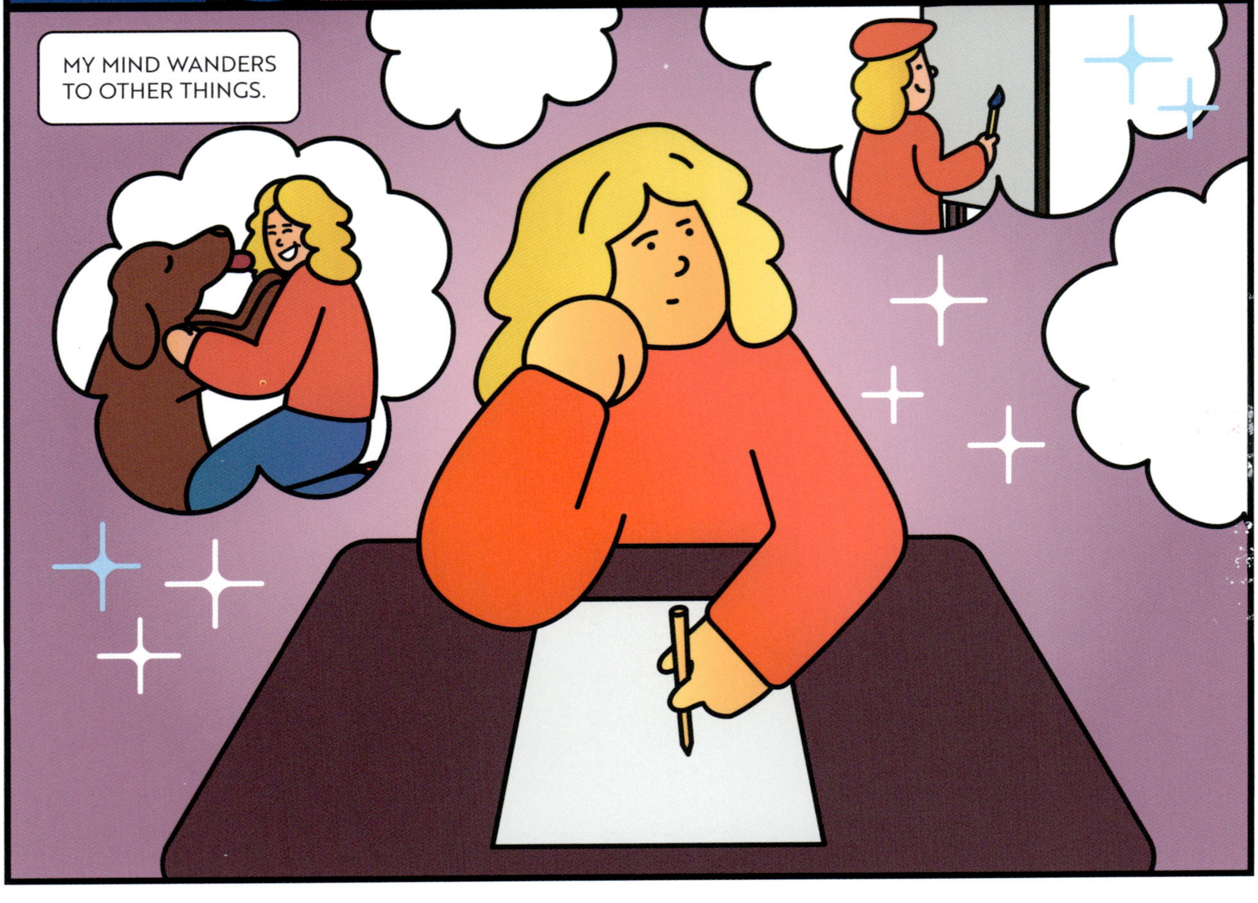
MY MIND WANDERS TO OTHER THINGS.

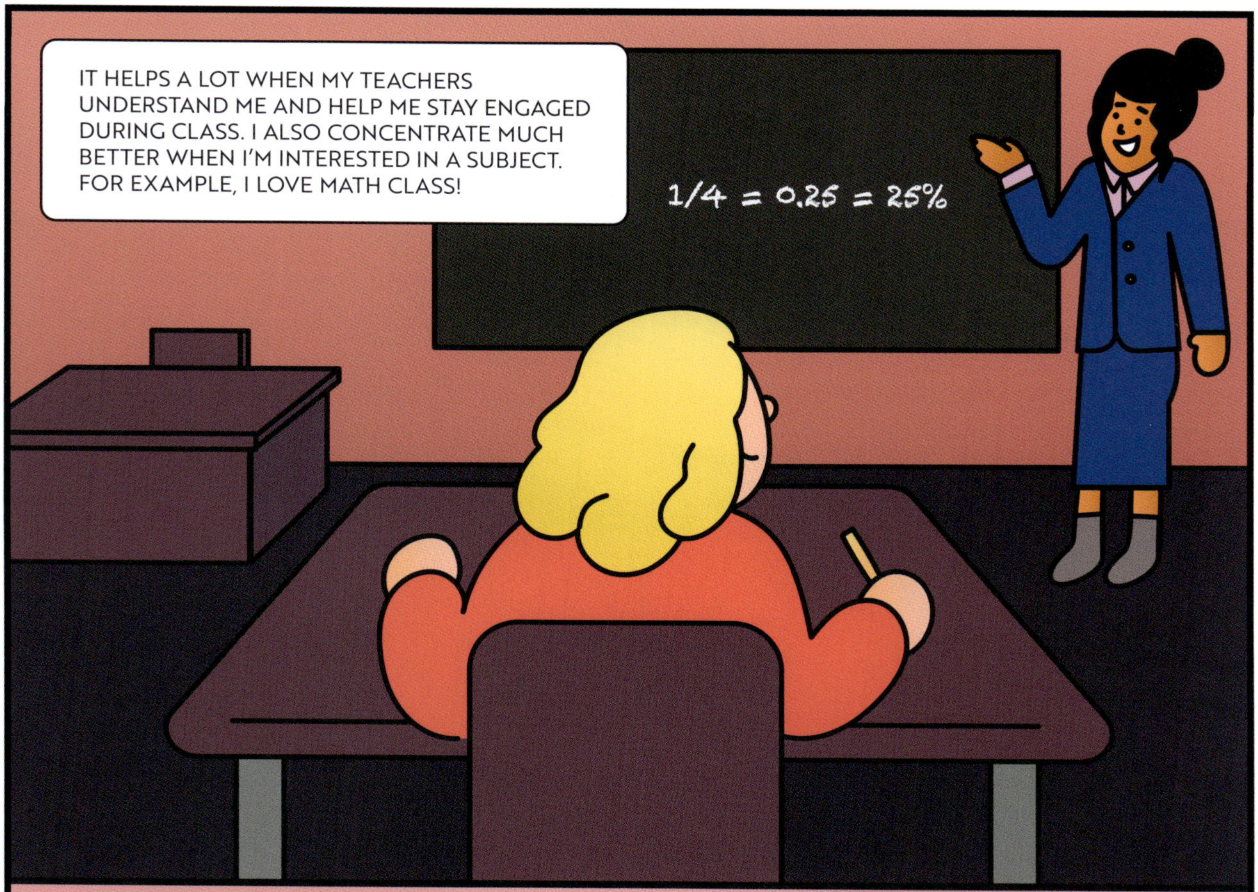
IT HELPS A LOT WHEN MY TEACHERS UNDERSTAND ME AND HELP ME STAY ENGAGED DURING CLASS. I ALSO CONCENTRATE MUCH BETTER WHEN I'M INTERESTED IN A SUBJECT. FOR EXAMPLE, I LOVE MATH CLASS!
1/4 = 0.25 = 25%

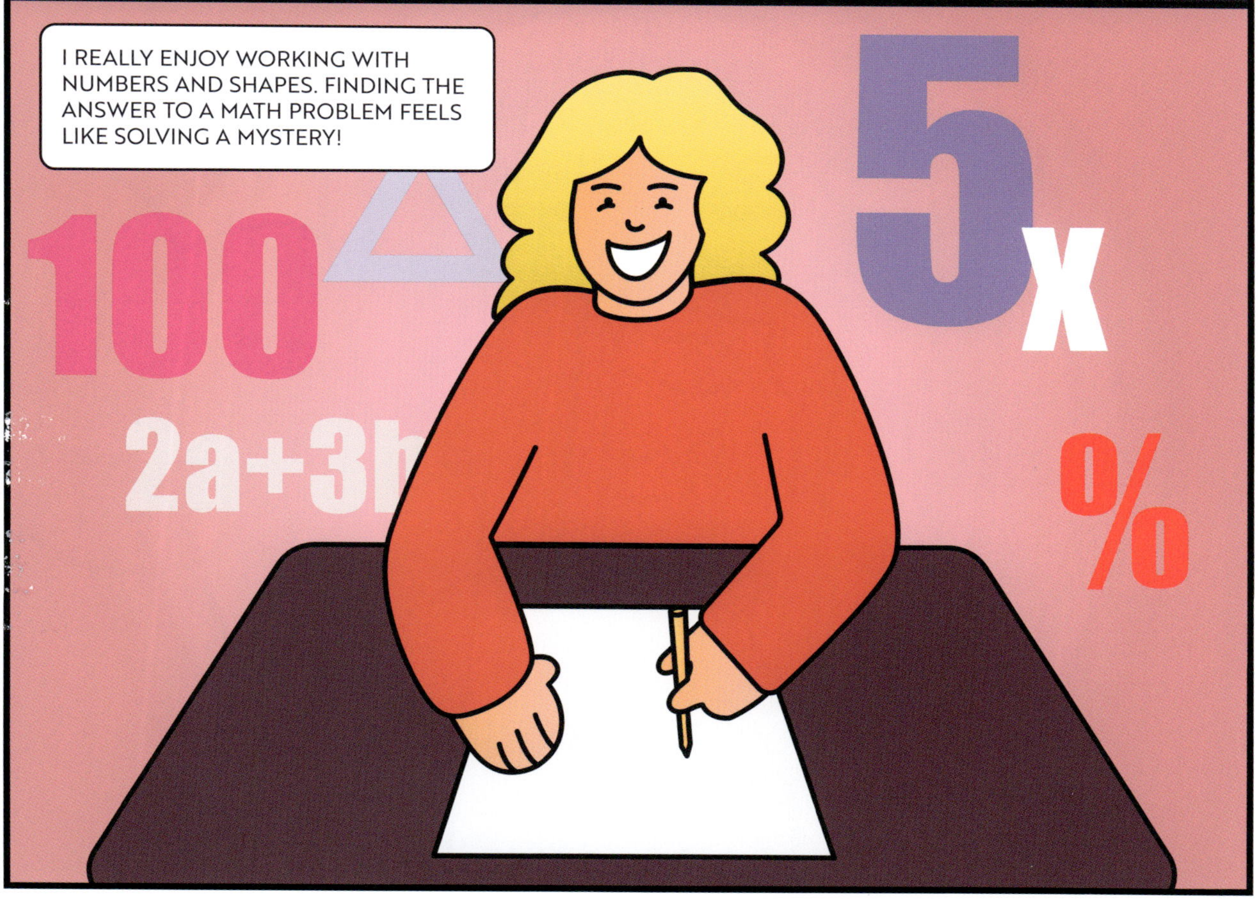
I REALLY ENJOY WORKING WITH NUMBERS AND SHAPES. FINDING THE ANSWER TO A MATH PROBLEM FEELS LIKE SOLVING A MYSTERY!
100
5
x
2a+3b
%

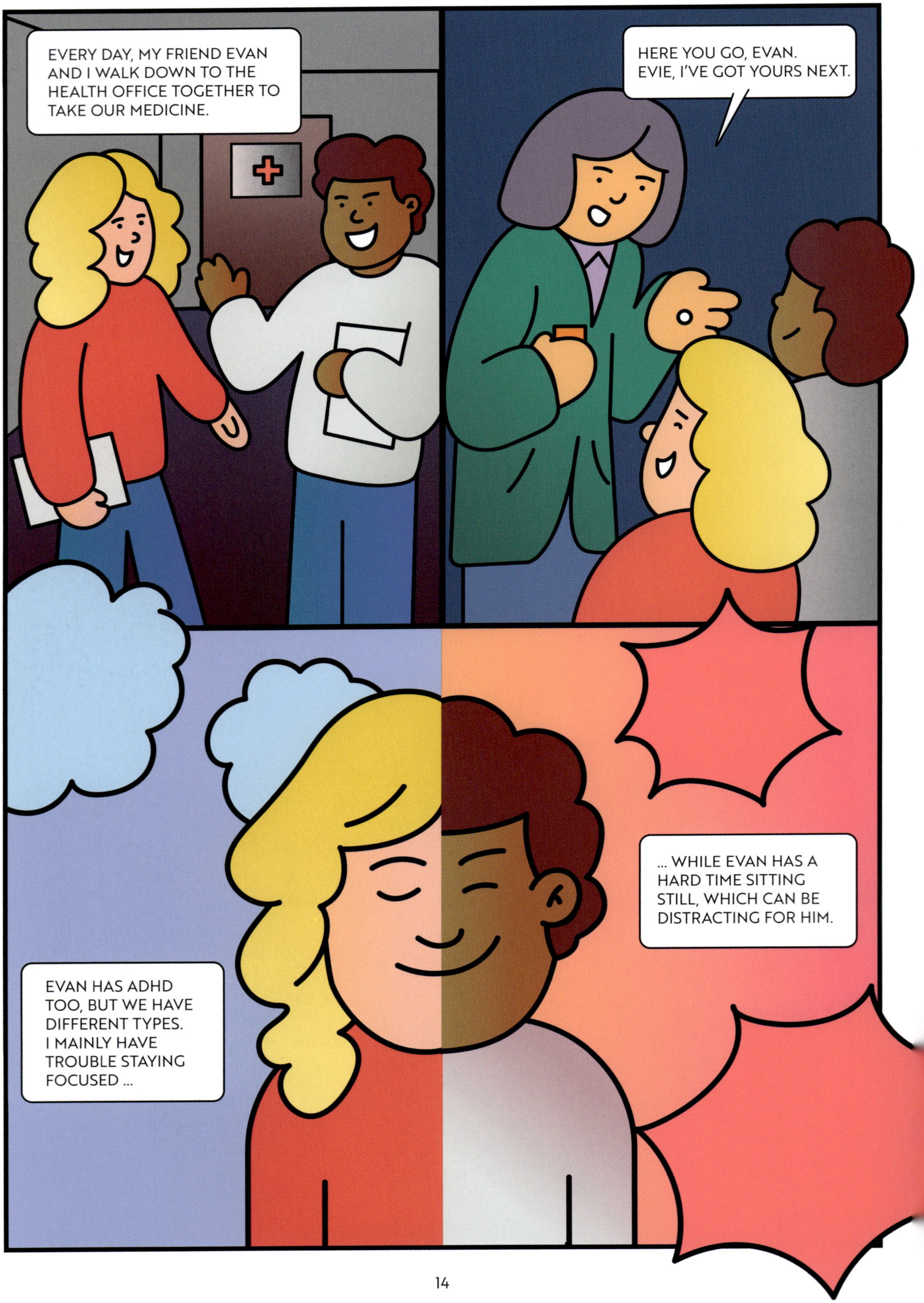
EVERY DAY, MY FRIEND EVAN AND I WALK DOWN TO THE HEALTH OFFICE TOGETHER TO TAKE OUR MEDICINE.
HERE YOU GO, EVAN. EVIE, I'VE GOT YOURS NEXT.
EVAN HAS ADHD TOO, BUT WE HAVE DIFFERENT TYPES. I MAINLY HAVE TROUBLE STAYING FOCUSED ...
... WHILE EVAN HAS A HARD TIME SITTING STILL, WHICH CAN BE DISTRACTING FOR HIM.

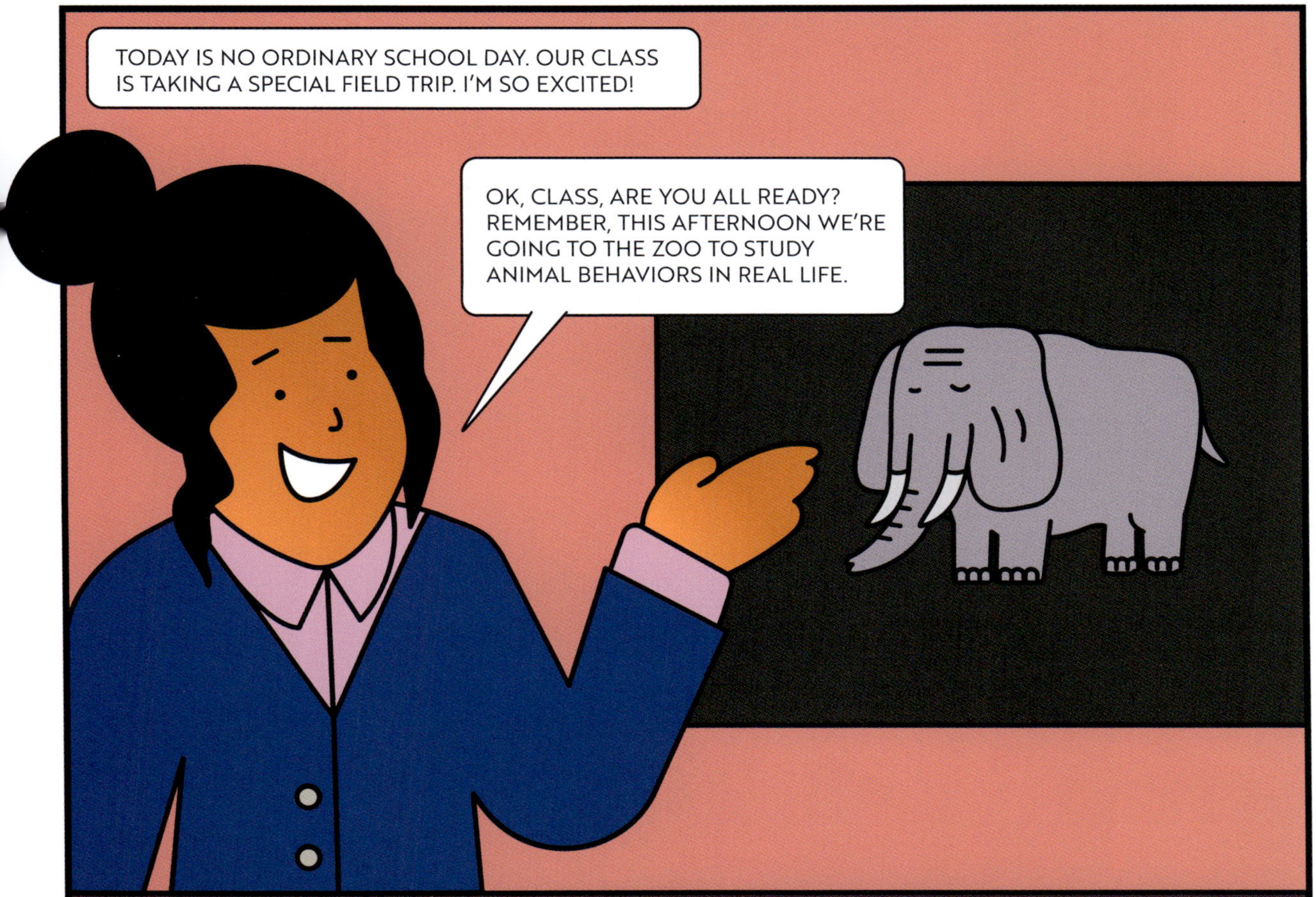
TODAY IS NO ORDINARY SCHOOL DAY. OUR CLASS IS TAKING A SPECIAL FIELD TRIP. I'M SO EXCITED!
OK, CLASS, ARE YOU ALL READY? REMEMBER, THIS AFTERNOON WE'RE GOING TO THE ZOO TO STUDY ANIMAL BEHAVIORS IN REAL LIFE.

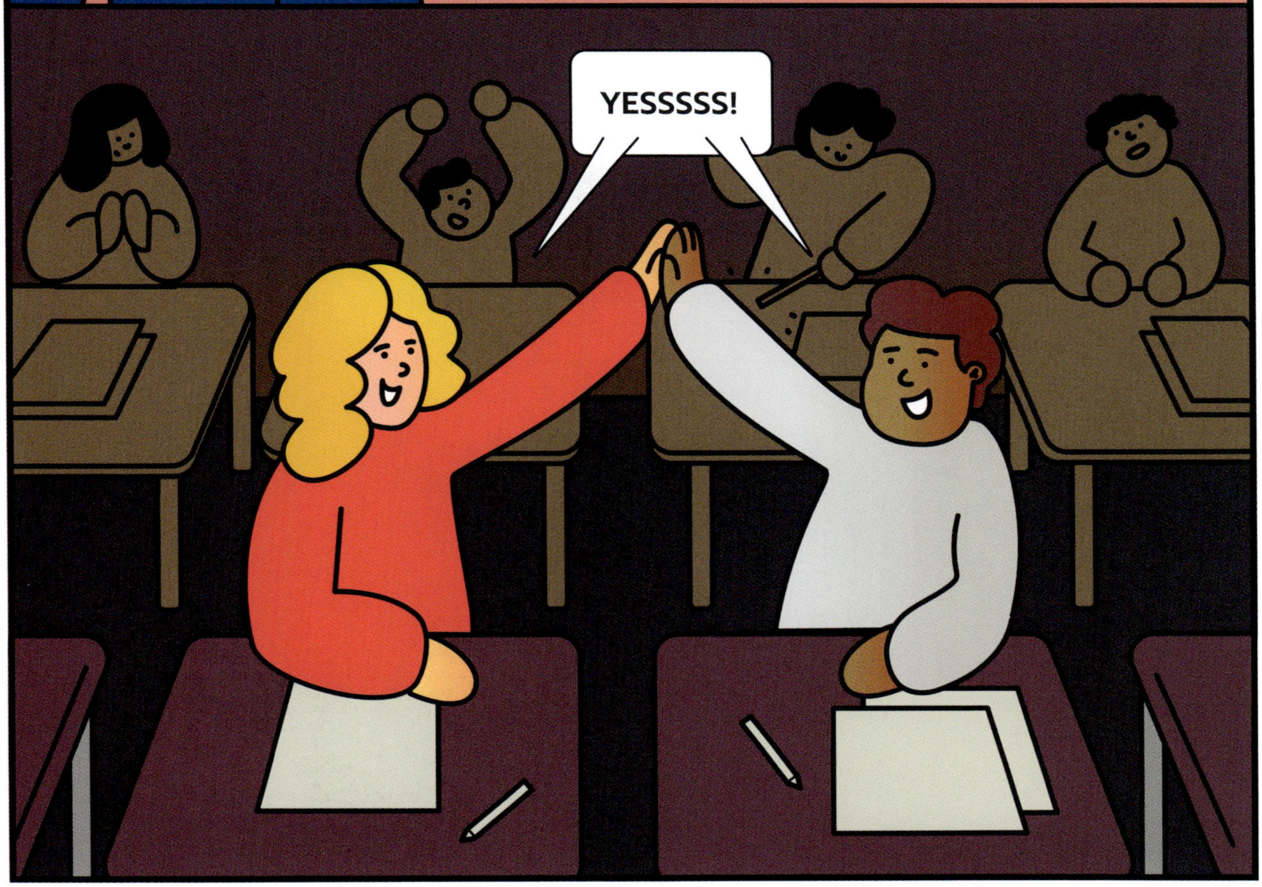
YESSSSS!

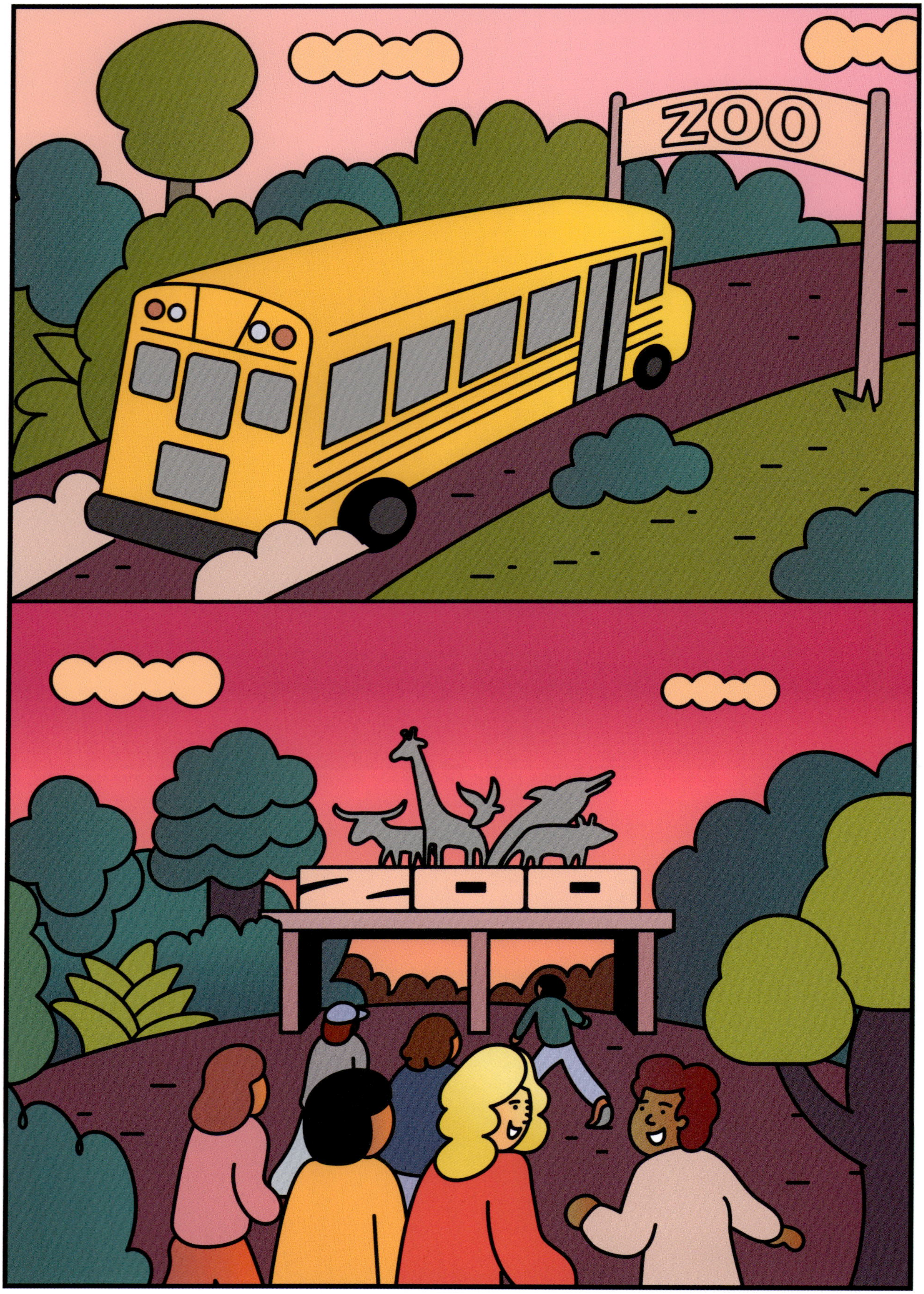
ZOO
ZOO

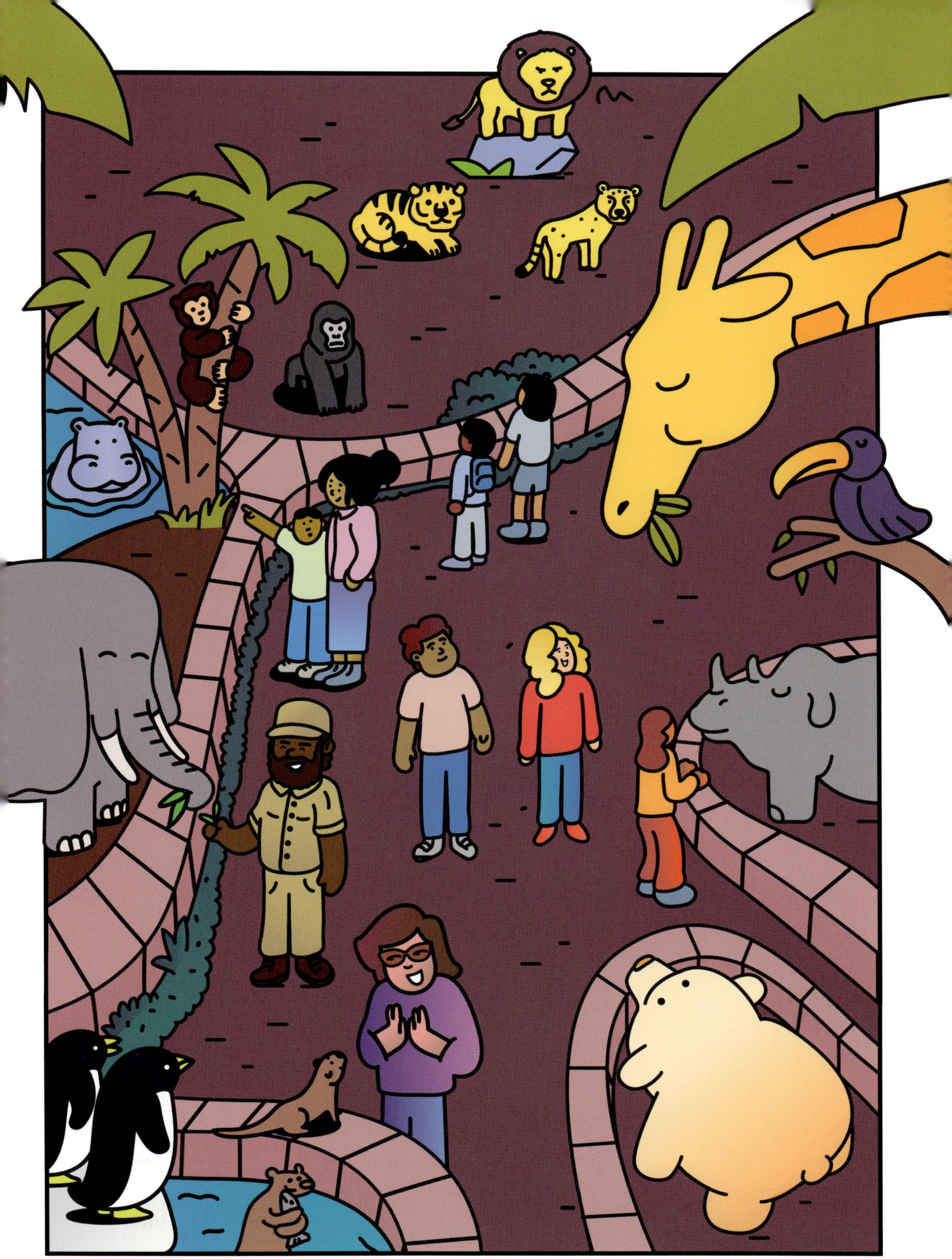

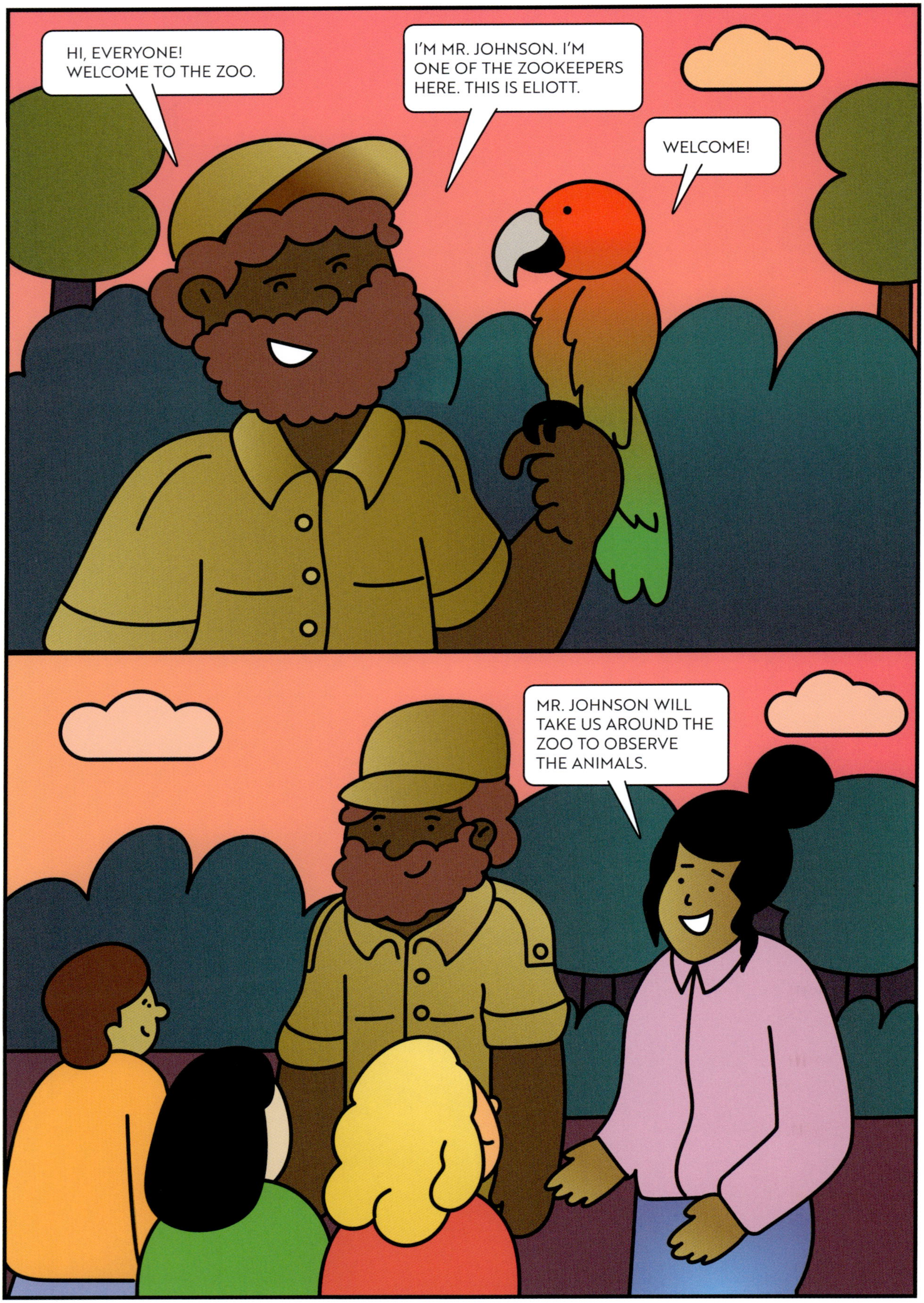
HI, EVERYONE! WELCOME TO THE ZOO.
I'M MR. JOHNSON. I'M ONE OF THE ZOOKEEPERS HERE. THIS IS ELIOTT.
WELCOME!
MR. JOHNSON WILL TAKE US AROUND THE ZOO TO OBSERVE THE ANIMALS.

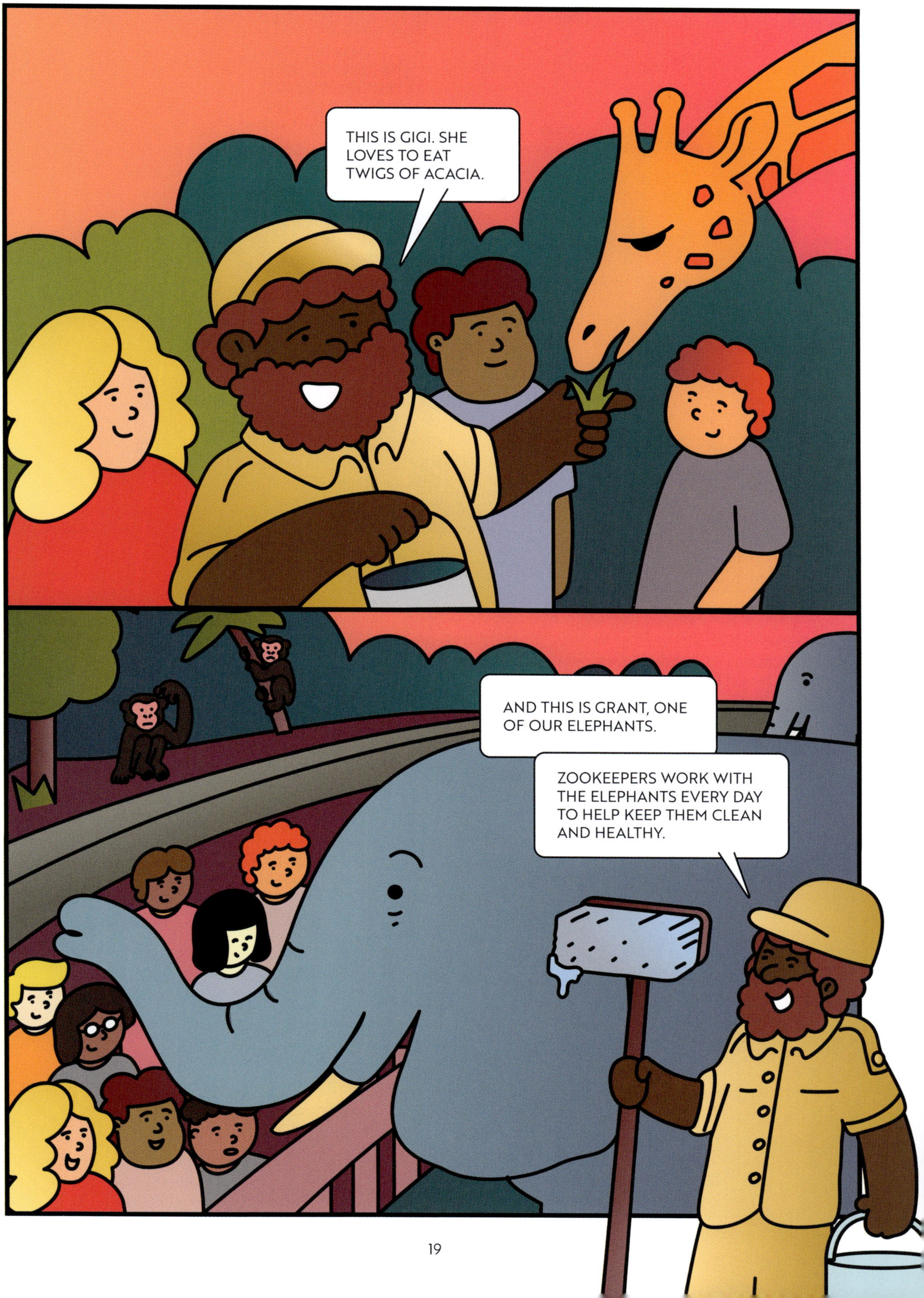
THIS IS GIGI. SHE LOVES TO EAT TWIGS OF ACACIA.
AND THIS IS GRANT, ONE OF OUR ELEPHANTS.
ZOOKEEPERS WORK WITH THE ELEPHANTS EVERY DAY TO HELP KEEP THEM CLEAN AND HEALTHY.

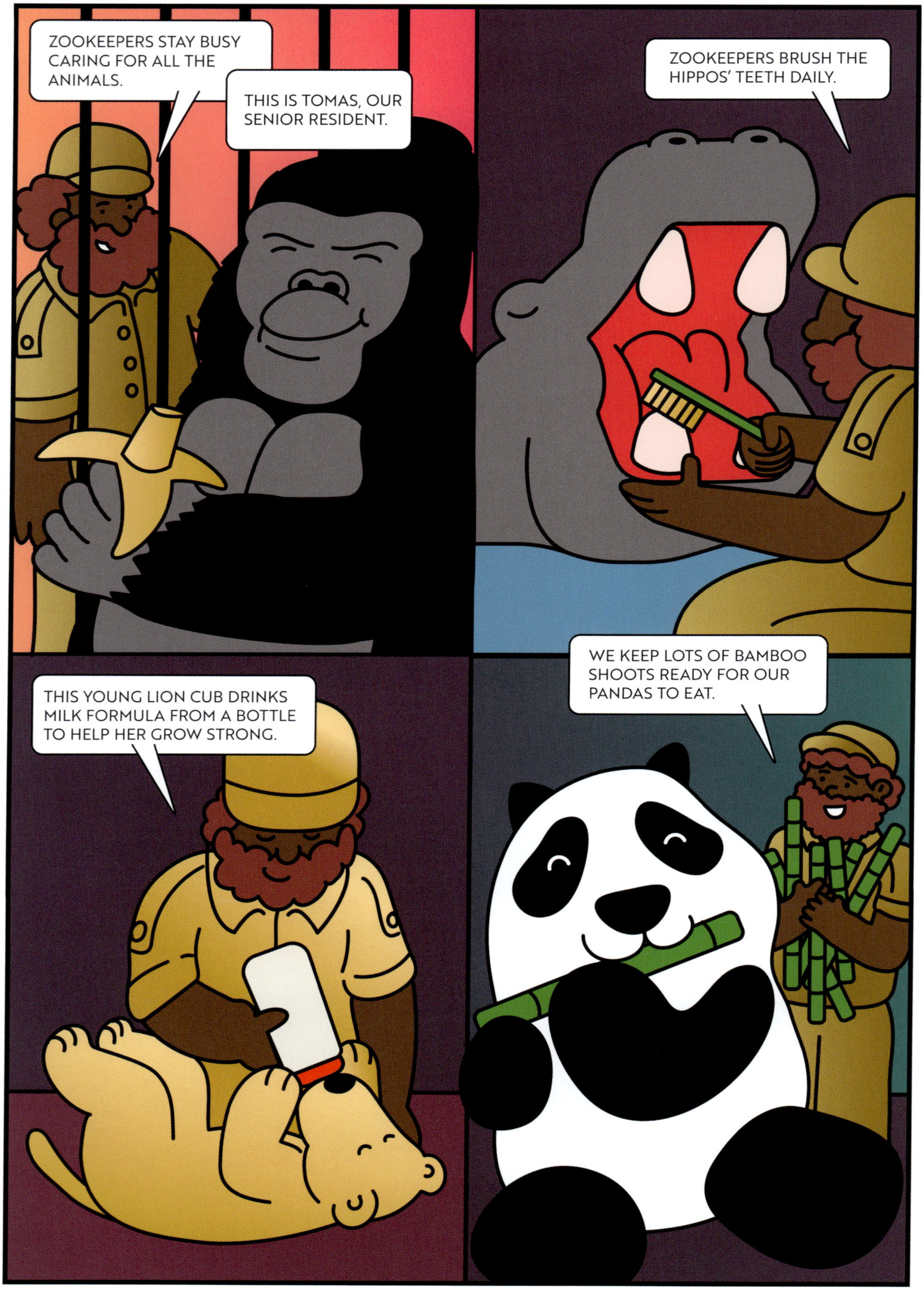
ZOOKEEPERS STAY BUSY CARING FOR ALL THE ANIMALS.
THIS IS TOMAS, OUR SENIOR RESIDENT.
ZOOKEEPERS BRUSH THE HIPPOS' TEETH DAILY.
THIS YOUNG LION CUB DRINKS MILK FORMULA FROM A BOTTLE TO HELP HER GROW STRONG.
WE KEEP LOTS OF BAMBOO SHOOTS READY FOR OUR PANDAS TO EAT.

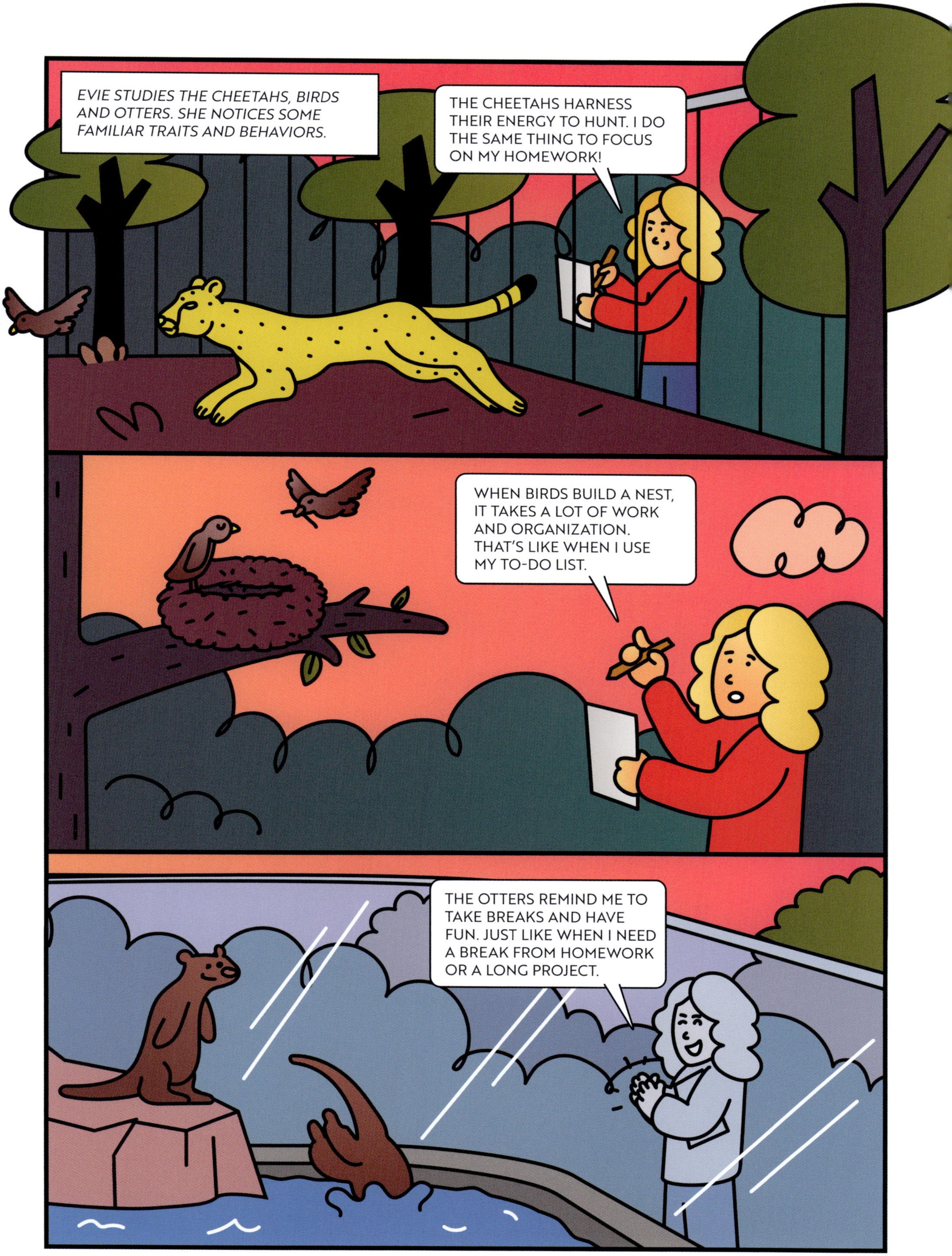
EVIE STUDIES THE CHEETAHS, BIRDS AND OTTERS. SHE NOTICES SOME FAMILIAR TRAITS AND BEHAVIORS.
THE CHEETAHS HARNESS THEIR ENERGY TO HUNT. I DO THE SAME THING TO FOCUS ON MY HOMEWORK!
WHEN BIRDS BUILD A NEST, IT TAKES A LOT OF WORK AND ORGANIZATION. THAT'S LIKE WHEN I USE MY TO-DO LIST.
THE OTTERS REMIND ME TO TAKE BREAKS AND HAVE FUN. JUST LIKE WHEN I NEED A BREAK FROM HOMEWORK OR A LONG PROJECT.

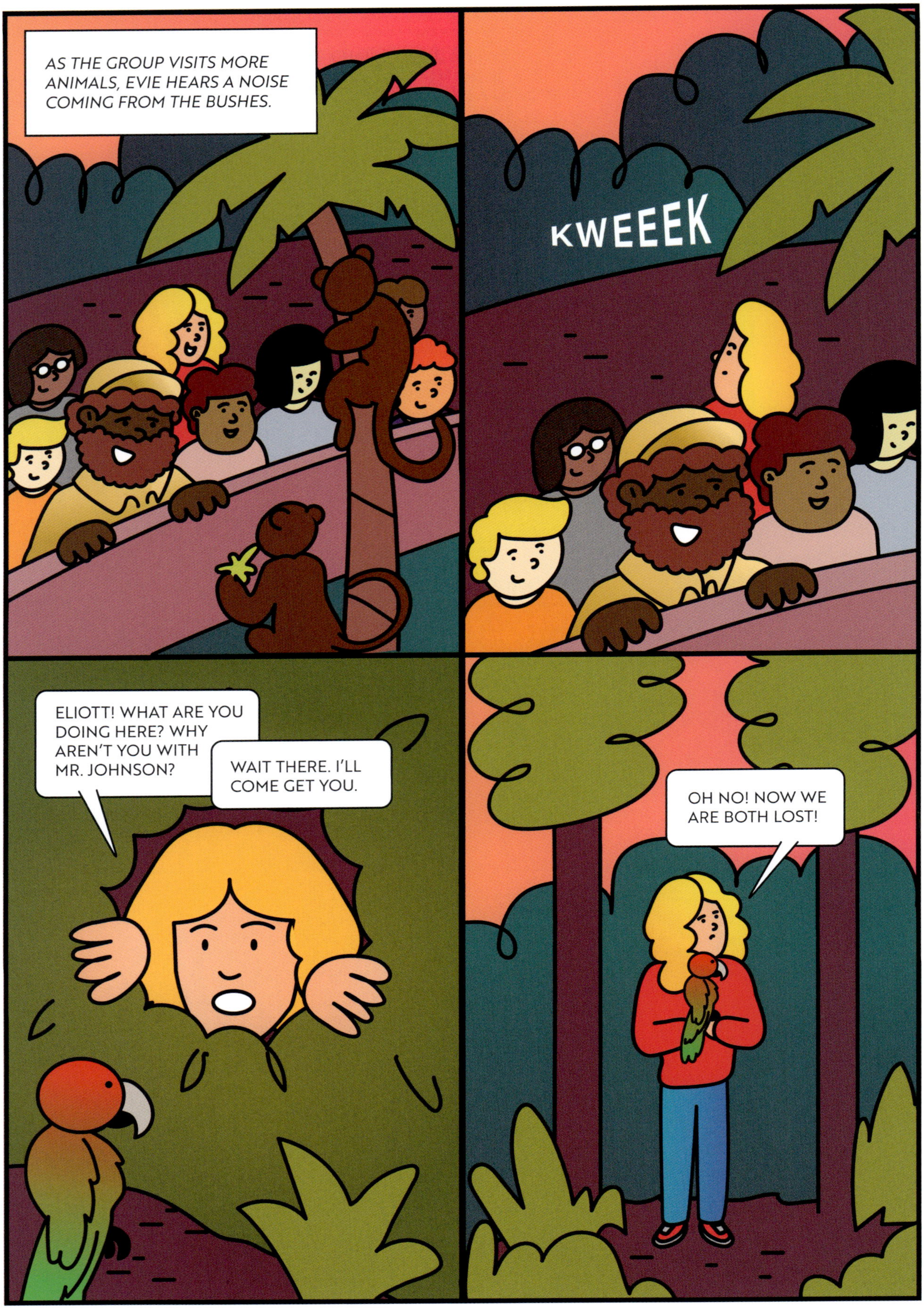
AS THE GROUP VISITS MORE ANIMALS, EVIE HEARS A NOISE COMING FROM THE BUSHES.
KWEEEK
ELIOTT! WHAT ARE YOU DOING HERE? WHY AREN'T YOU WITH MR. JOHNSON?
WAIT THERE. I'LL COME GET YOU.
OH NO! NOW WE ARE BOTH LOST!

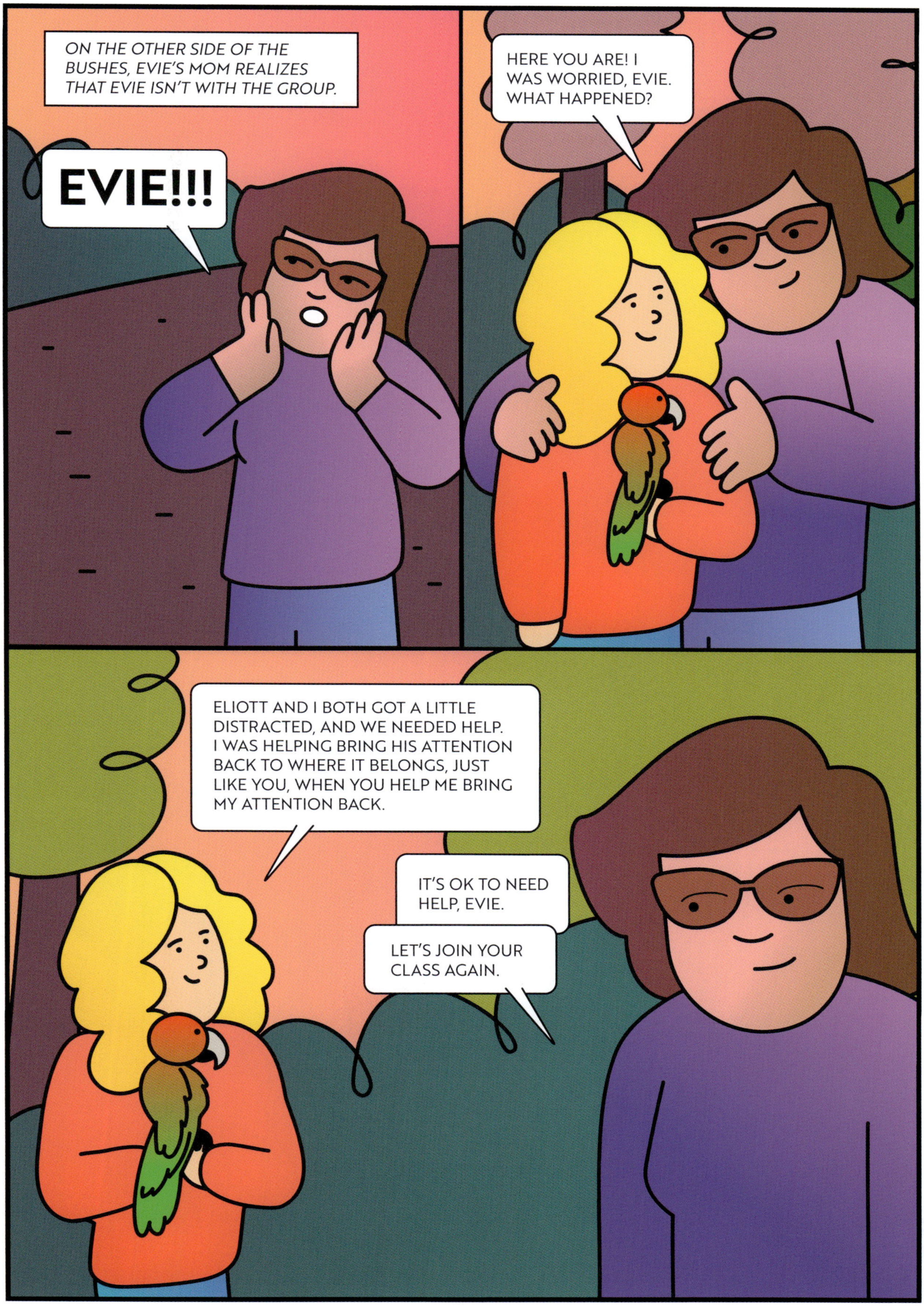
ON THE OTHER SIDE OF THE BUSHES, EVIE'S MOM REALIZES THAT EVIE ISN'T WITH THE GROUP.
EVIE!!!
HERE YOU ARE! I WAS WORRIED, EVIE. WHAT HAPPENED?
ELIOTT AND I BOTH GOT A LITTLE DISTRACTED, AND WE NEEDED HELP. I WAS HELPING BRING HIS ATTENTION BACK TO WHERE IT BELONGS, JUST LIKE YOU, WHEN YOU HELP ME BRING MY ATTENTION BACK.
IT'S OK TO NEED HELP, EVIE.
LET'S JOIN YOUR CLASS AGAIN.

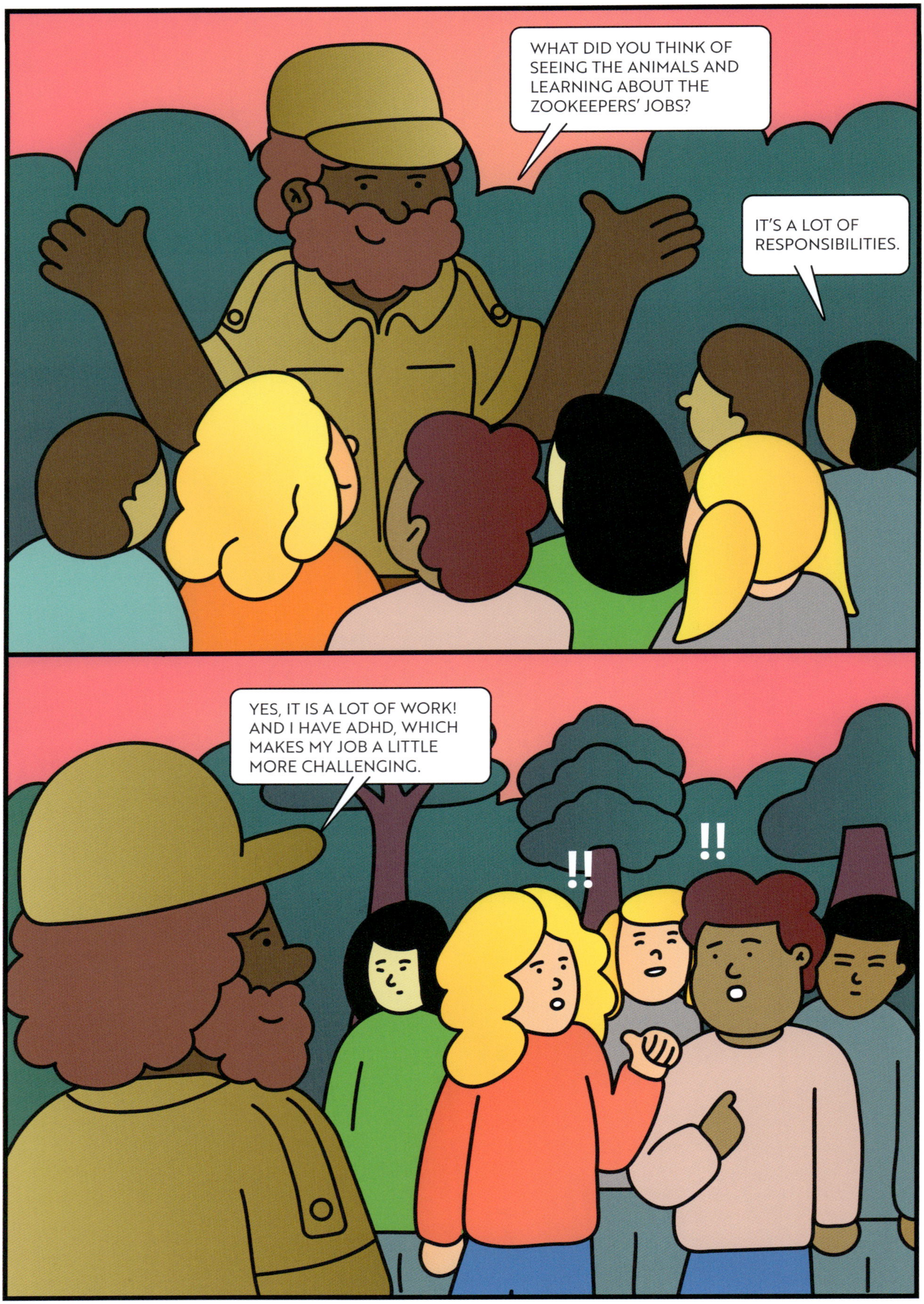
WHAT DID YOU THINK OF SEEING THE ANIMALS AND LEARNING ABOUT THE ZOOKEEPERS' JOBS?
IT'S A LOT OF RESPONSIBILITIES.
YES, IT IS A LOT OF WORK! AND I HAVE ADHD, WHICH MAKES MY JOB A LITTLE MORE CHALLENGING.
!!
!!

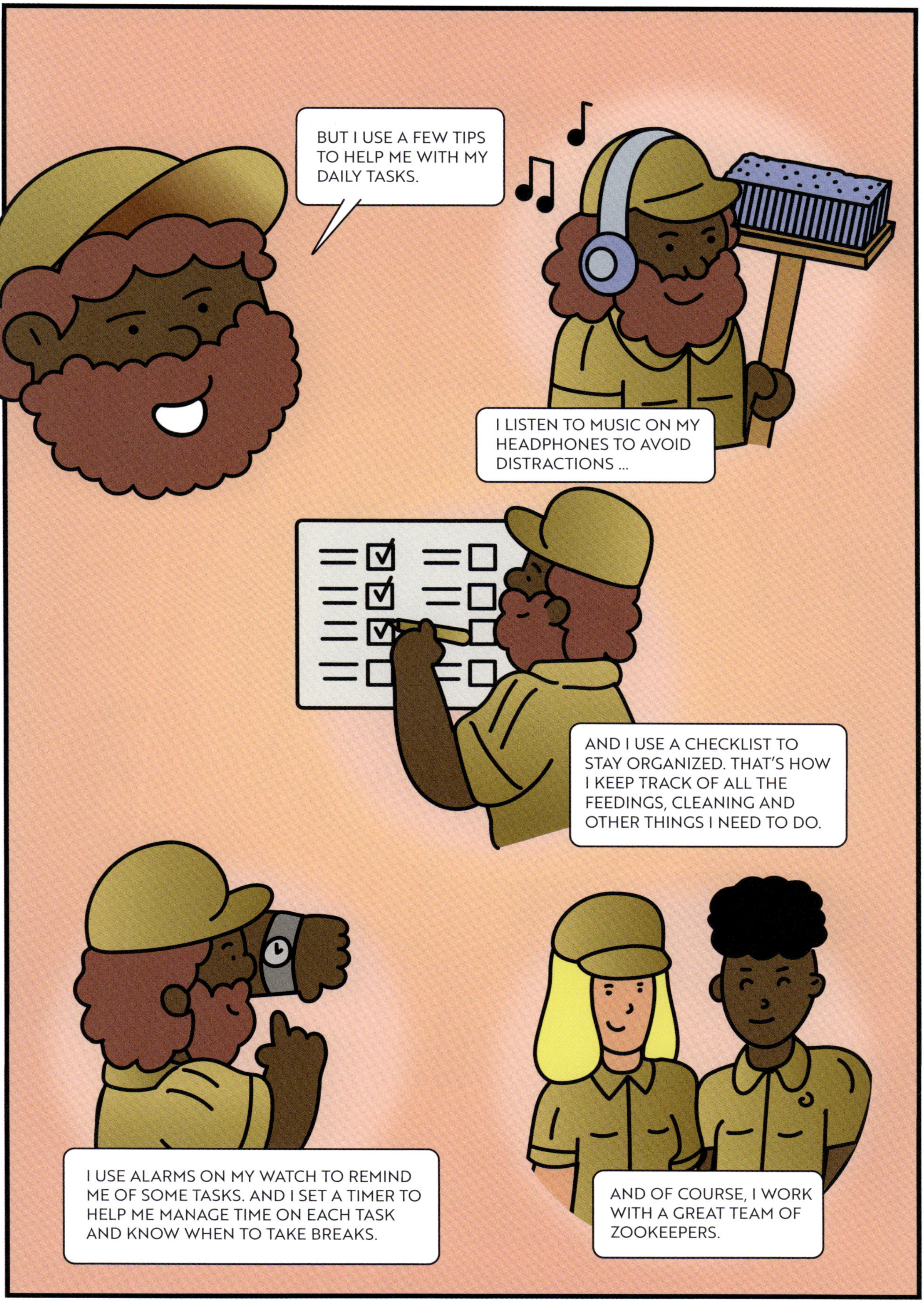
BUT I USE A FEW TIPS TO HELP ME WITH MY DAILY TASKS.
I LISTEN TO MUSIC ON MY HEADPHONES TO AVOID DISTRACTIONS ...
AND I USE A CHECKLIST TO STAY ORGANIZED. THAT'S HOW I KEEP TRACK OF ALL THE FEEDINGS, CLEANING AND OTHER THINGS I NEED TO DO.
I USE ALARMS ON MY WATCH TO REMIND ME OF SOME TASKS. AND I SET A TIMER TO HELP ME MANAGE TIME ON EACH TASK AND KNOW WHEN TO TAKE BREAKS.
AND OF COURSE, I WORK WITH A GREAT TEAM OF ZOOKEEPERS.

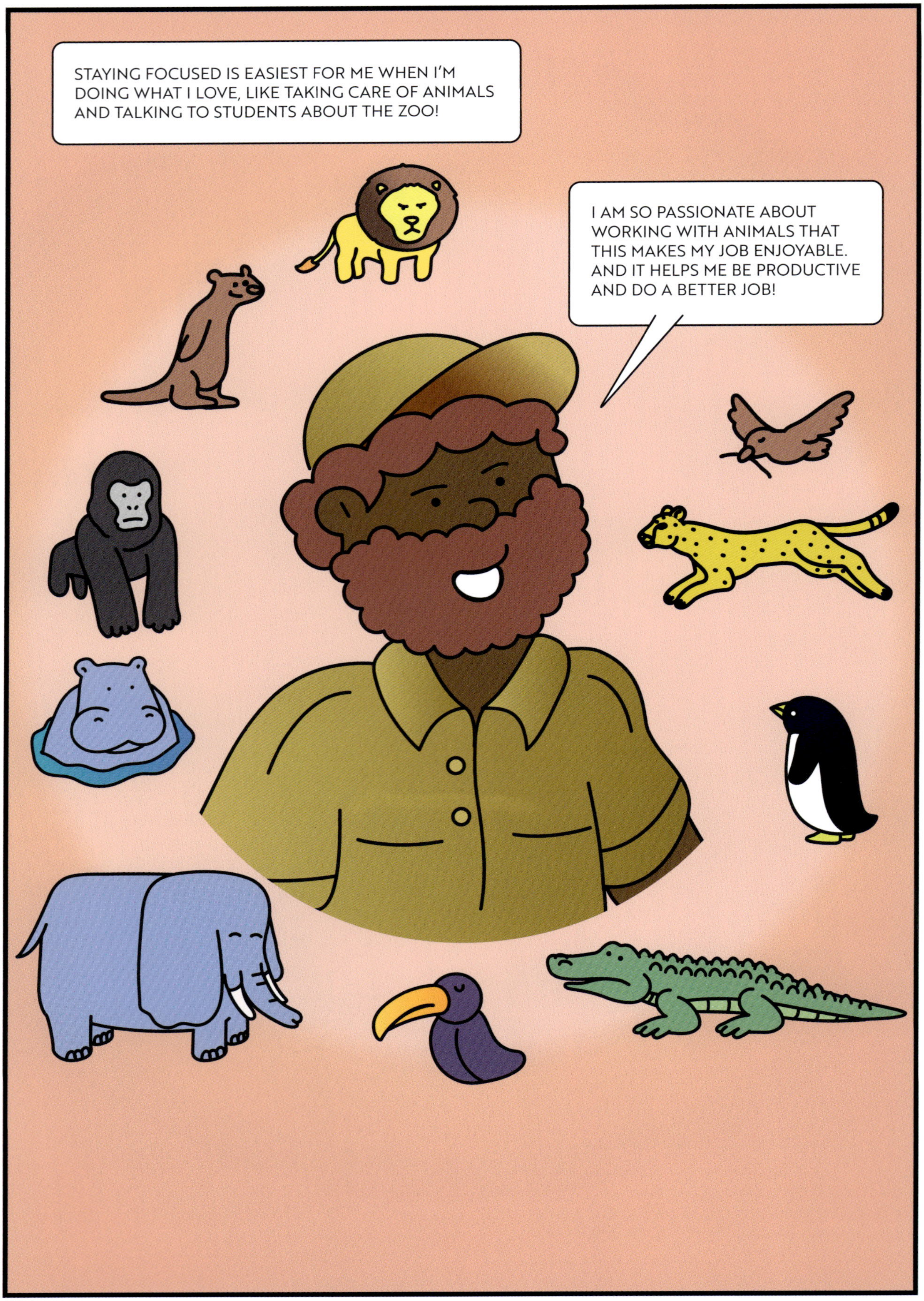
STAYING FOCUSED IS EASIEST FOR ME WHEN I'M DOING WHAT I LOVE, LIKE TAKING CARE OF ANIMALS AND TALKING TO STUDENTS ABOUT THE ZOO!
I AM SO PASSIONATE ABOUT WORKING WITH ANIMALS THAT THIS MAKES MY JOB ENJOYABLE. AND IT HELPS ME BE PRODUCTIVE AND DO A BETTER JOB!

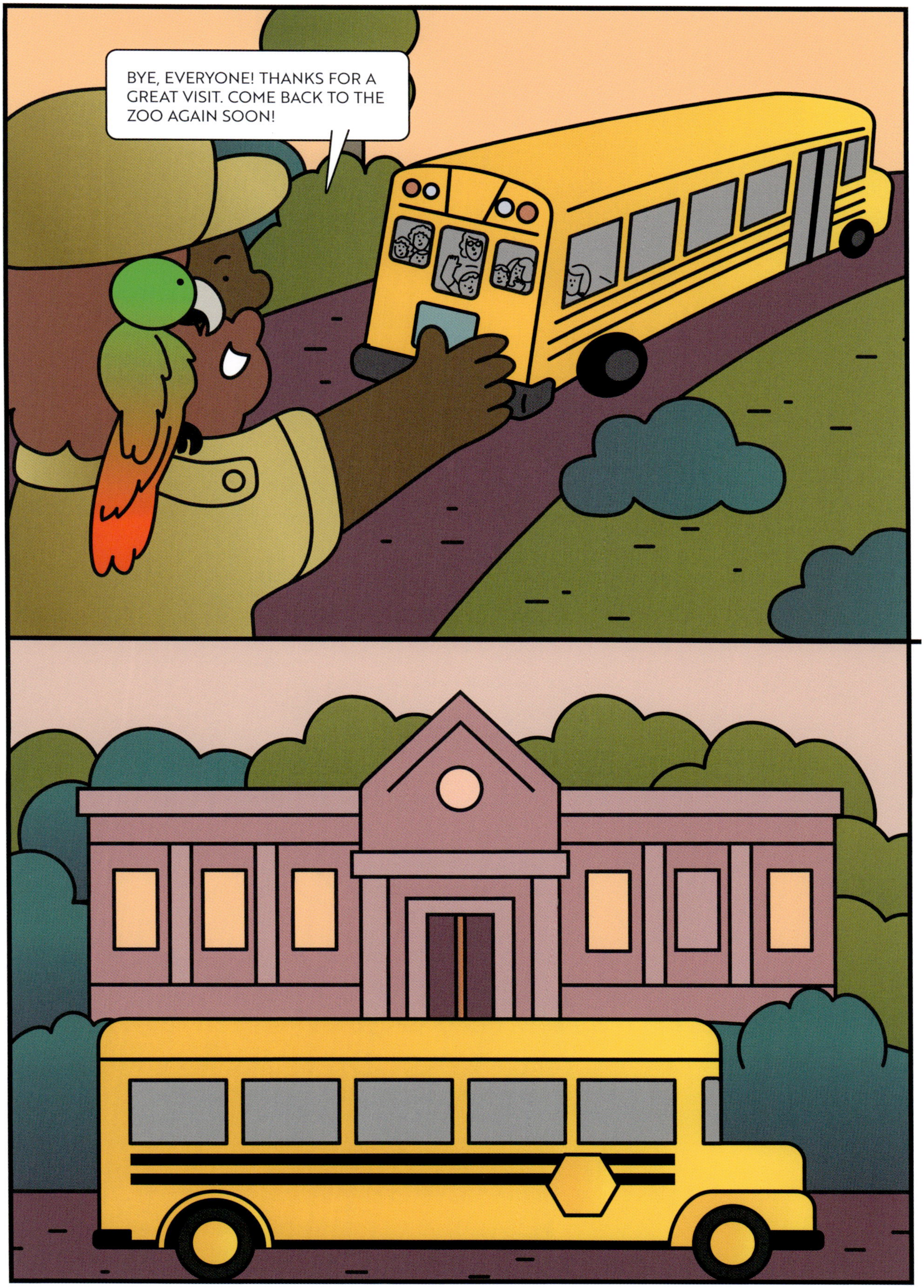
BYE, EVERYONE! THANKS FOR A GREAT VISIT. COME BACK TO THE ZOO AGAIN SOON!

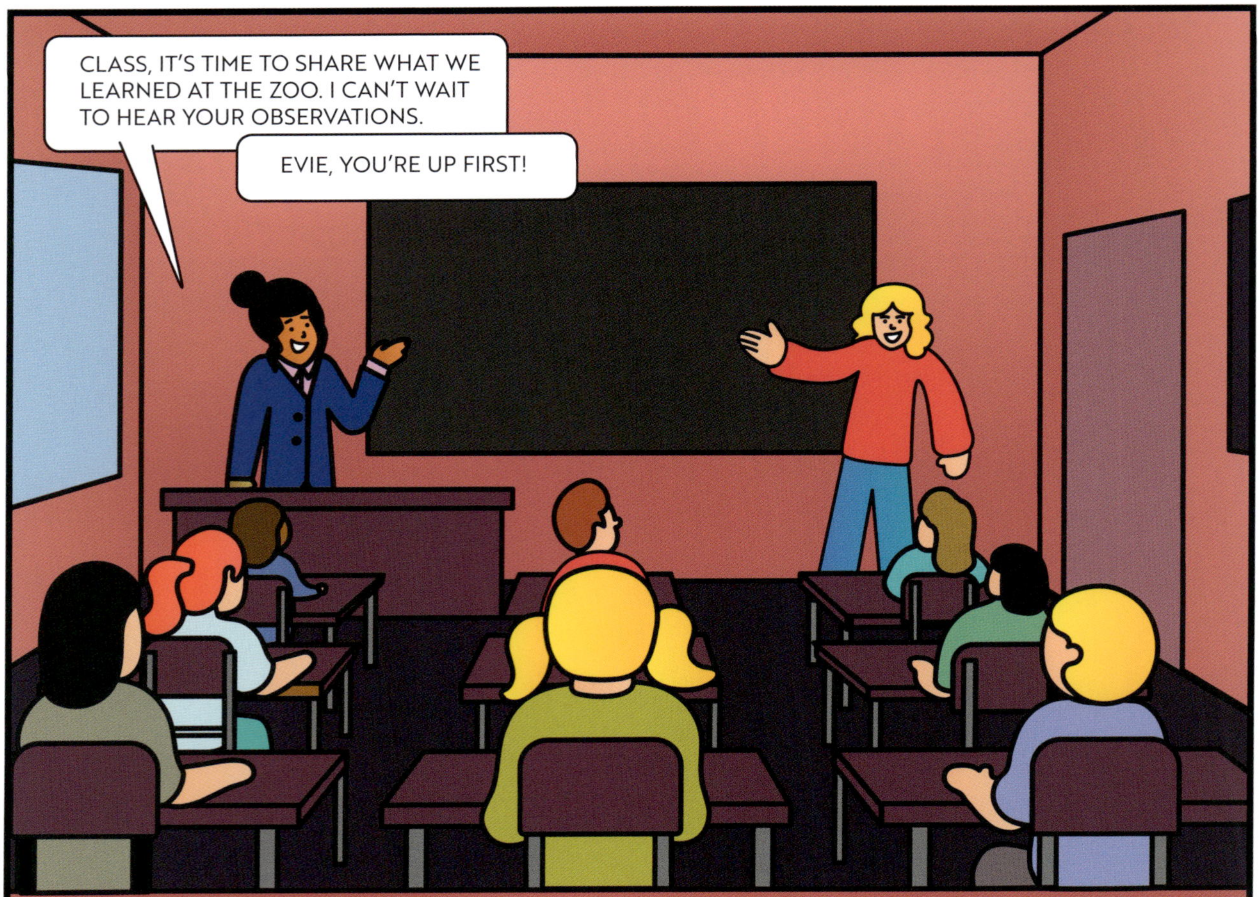
CLASS, IT'S TIME TO SHARE WHAT WE LEARNED AT THE ZOO. I CAN'T WAIT TO HEAR YOUR OBSERVATIONS.
EVIE, YOU'RE UP FIRST!

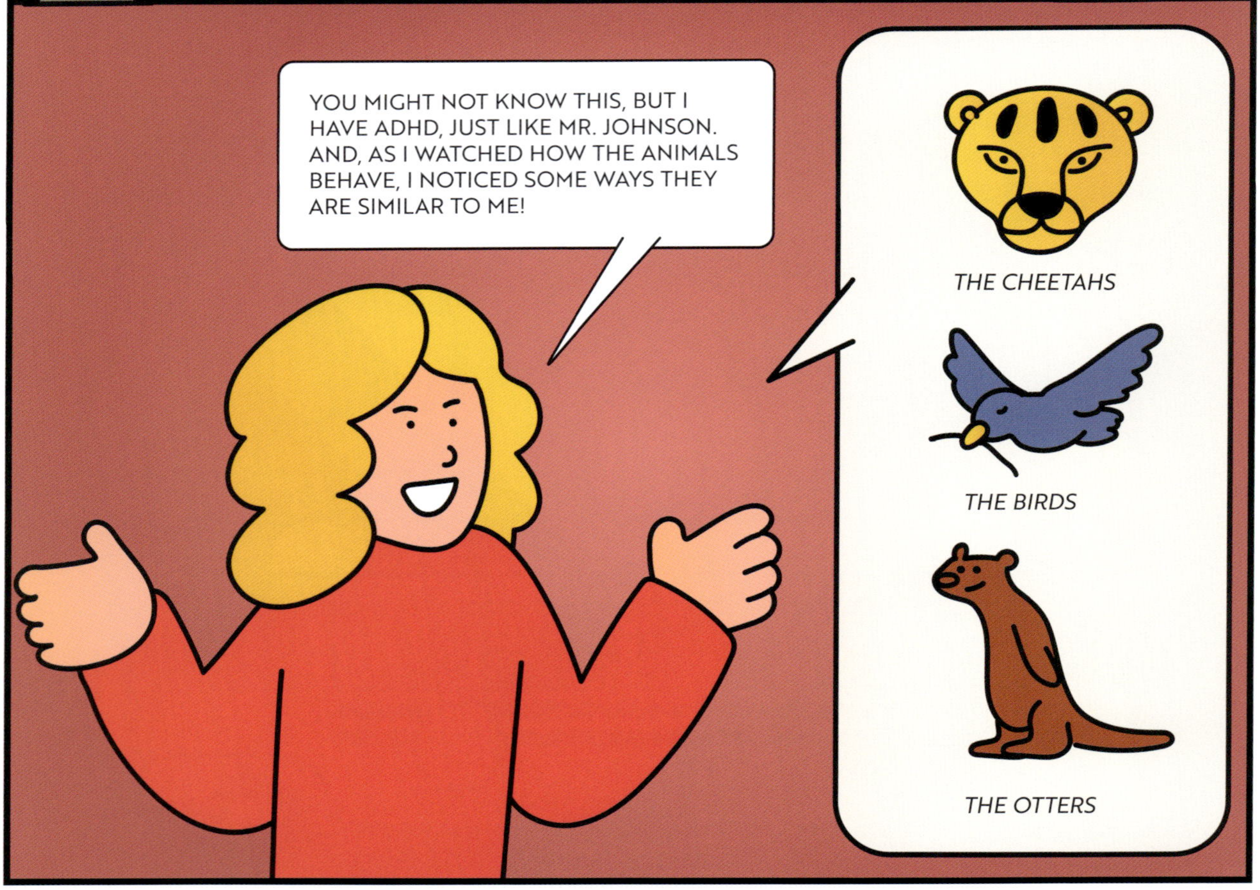
YOU MIGHT NOT KNOW THIS, BUT I HAVE ADHD, JUST LIKE MR. JOHNSON. AND, AS I WATCHED HOW THE ANIMALS BEHAVE, I NOTICED SOME WAYS THEY ARE SIMILAR TO ME!
THE CHEETAHS
THE BIRDS
THE OTTERS

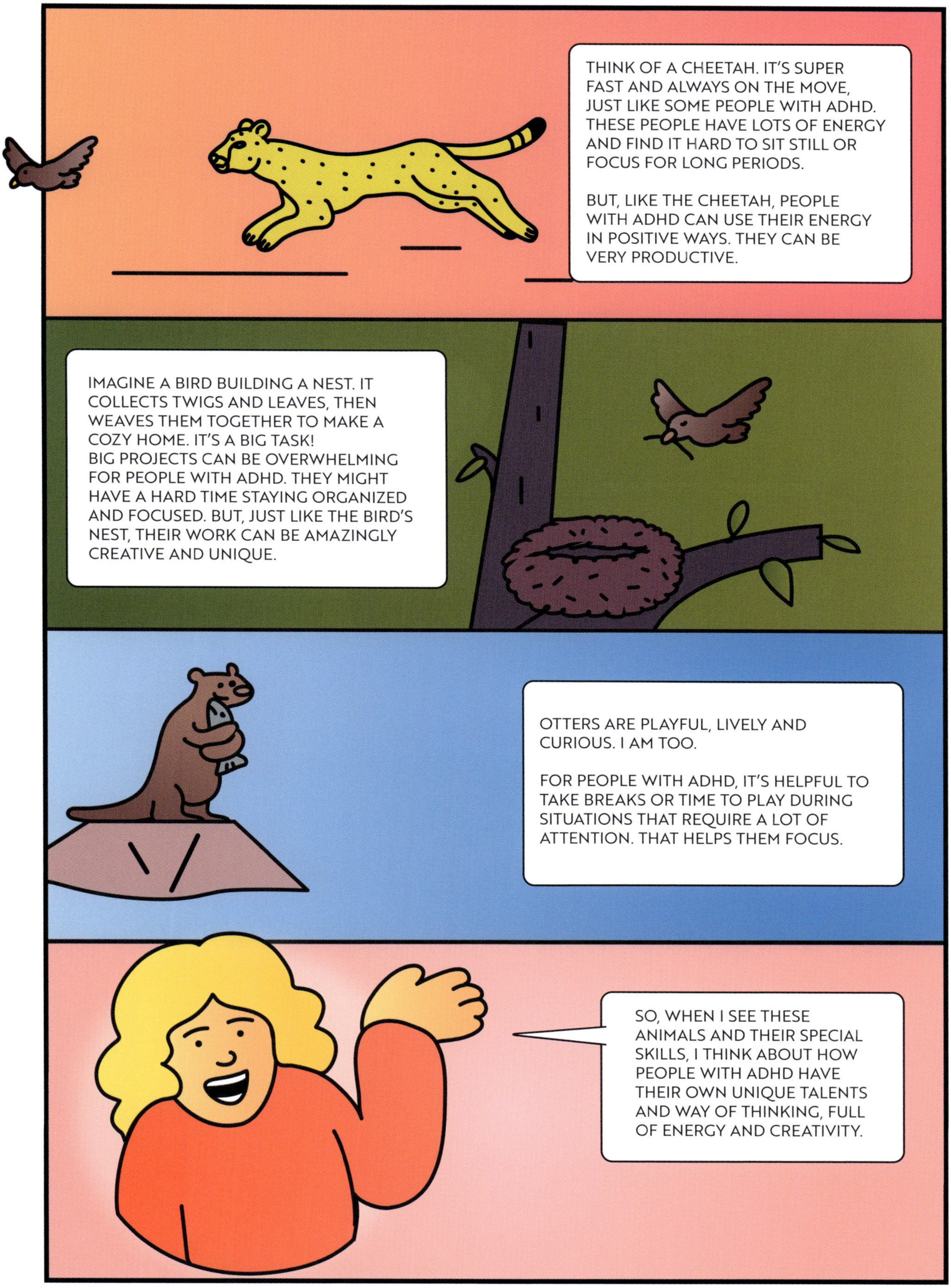
THINK OF A CHEETAH. IT'S SUPER FAST AND ALWAYS ON THE MOVE, JUST LIKE SOME PEOPLE WITH ADHD. THESE PEOPLE HAVE LOTS OF ENERGY AND FIND IT HARD TO SIT STILL OR FOCUS FOR LONG PERIODS.
BUT, LIKE THE CHEETAH, PEOPLE WITH ADHD CAN USE THEIR ENERGY IN POSITIVE WAYS. THEY CAN BE VERY PRODUCTIVE.
IMAGINE A BIRD BUILDING A NEST. IT COLLECTS TWIGS AND LEAVES, THEN WEAVES THEM TOGETHER TO MAKE A COZY HOME. IT'S A BIG TASK!
BIG PROJECTS CAN BE OVERWHELMING FOR PEOPLE WITH ADHD. THEY MIGHT HAVE A HARD TIME STAYING ORGANIZED AND FOCUSED. BUT, JUST LIKE THE BIRD'S NEST, THEIR WORK CAN BE AMAZINGLY CREATIVE AND UNIQUE.
OTTERS ARE PLAYFUL, LIVELY AND CURIOUS. I AM TOO.
FOR PEOPLE WITH ADHD, IT'S HELPFUL TO TAKE BREAKS OR TIME TO PLAY DURING SITUATIONS THAT REQUIRE A LOT OF ATTENTION. THAT HELPS THEM FOCUS.
SO, WHEN I SEE THESE ANIMALS AND THEIR SPECIAL SKILLS, I THINK ABOUT HOW PEOPLE WITH ADHD HAVE THEIR OWN UNIQUE TALENTS AND WAY OF THINKING, FULL OF ENERGY AND CREATIVITY.

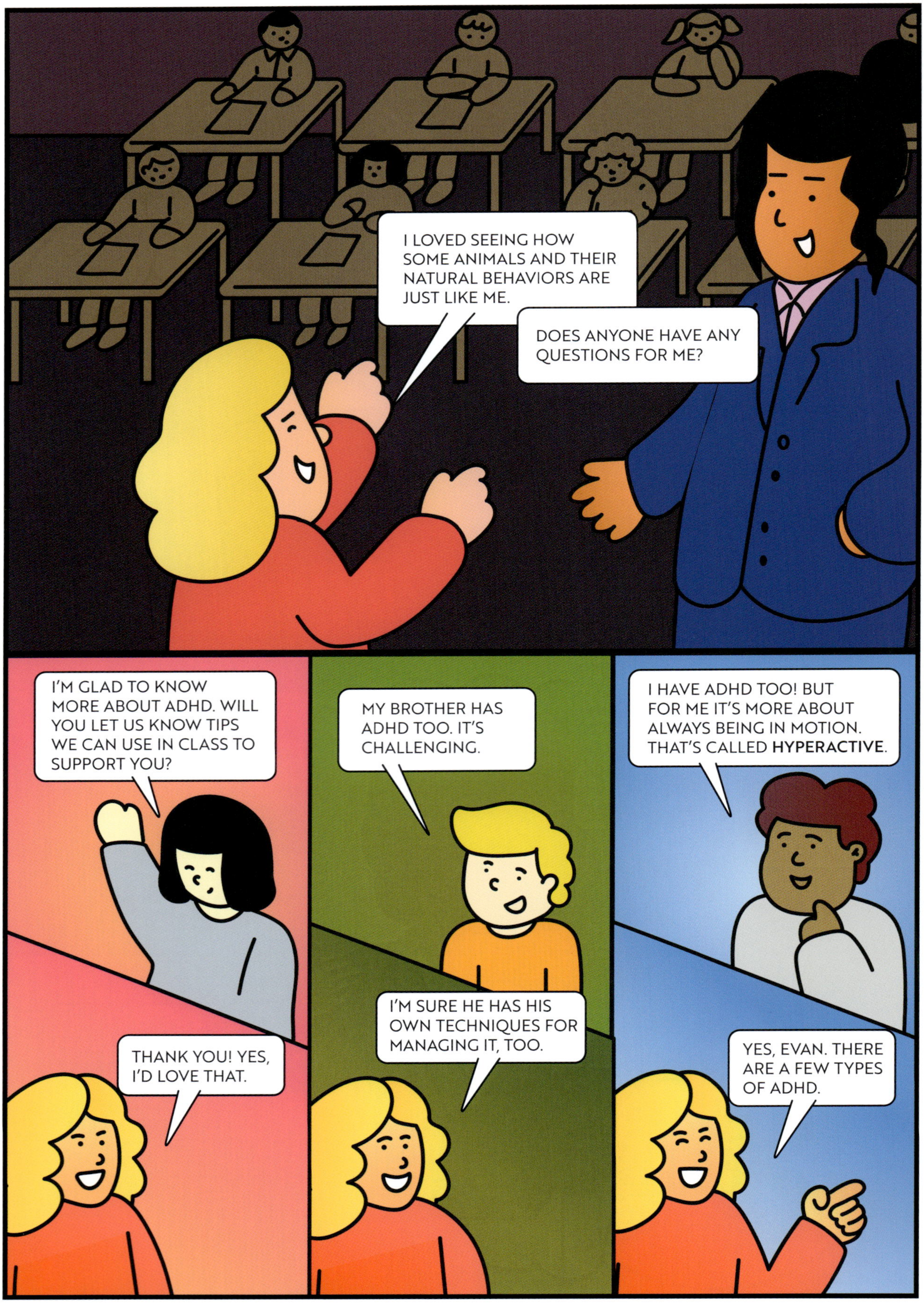
I LOVED SEEING HOW SOME ANIMALS AND THEIR NATURAL BEHAVIORS ARE JUST LIKE ME.
DOES ANYONE HAVE ANY QUESTIONS FOR ME?
I'M GLAD TO KNOW MORE ABOUT ADHD. WILL YOU LET US KNOW TIPS WE CAN USE IN CLASS TO SUPPORT YOU?
THANK YOU! YES, I'D LOVE THAT.
MY BROTHER HAS ADHD TOO. IT'S CHALLENGING.
I'M SURE HE HAS HIS OWN TECHNIQUES FOR MANAGING IT, TOO.
I HAVE ADHD TOO! BUT FOR ME IT'S MORE ABOUT ALWAYS BEING IN MOTION. THAT'S CALLED **HYPERACTIVE**.
YES, EVAN. THERE ARE A FEW TYPES OF ADHD.

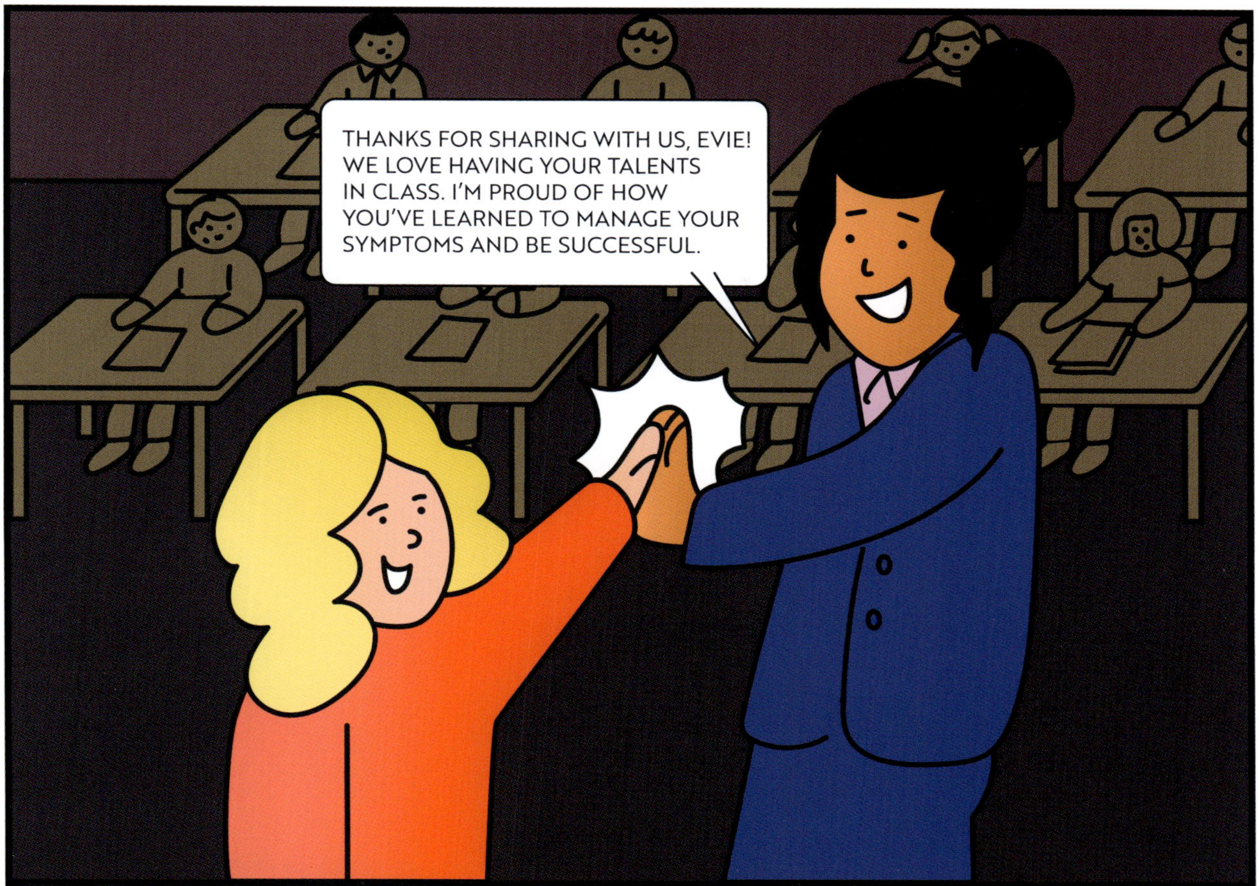
THANKS FOR SHARING WITH US, EVIE! WE LOVE HAVING YOUR TALENTS IN CLASS. I'M PROUD OF HOW YOU'VE LEARNED TO MANAGE YOUR SYMPTOMS AND BE SUCCESSFUL.

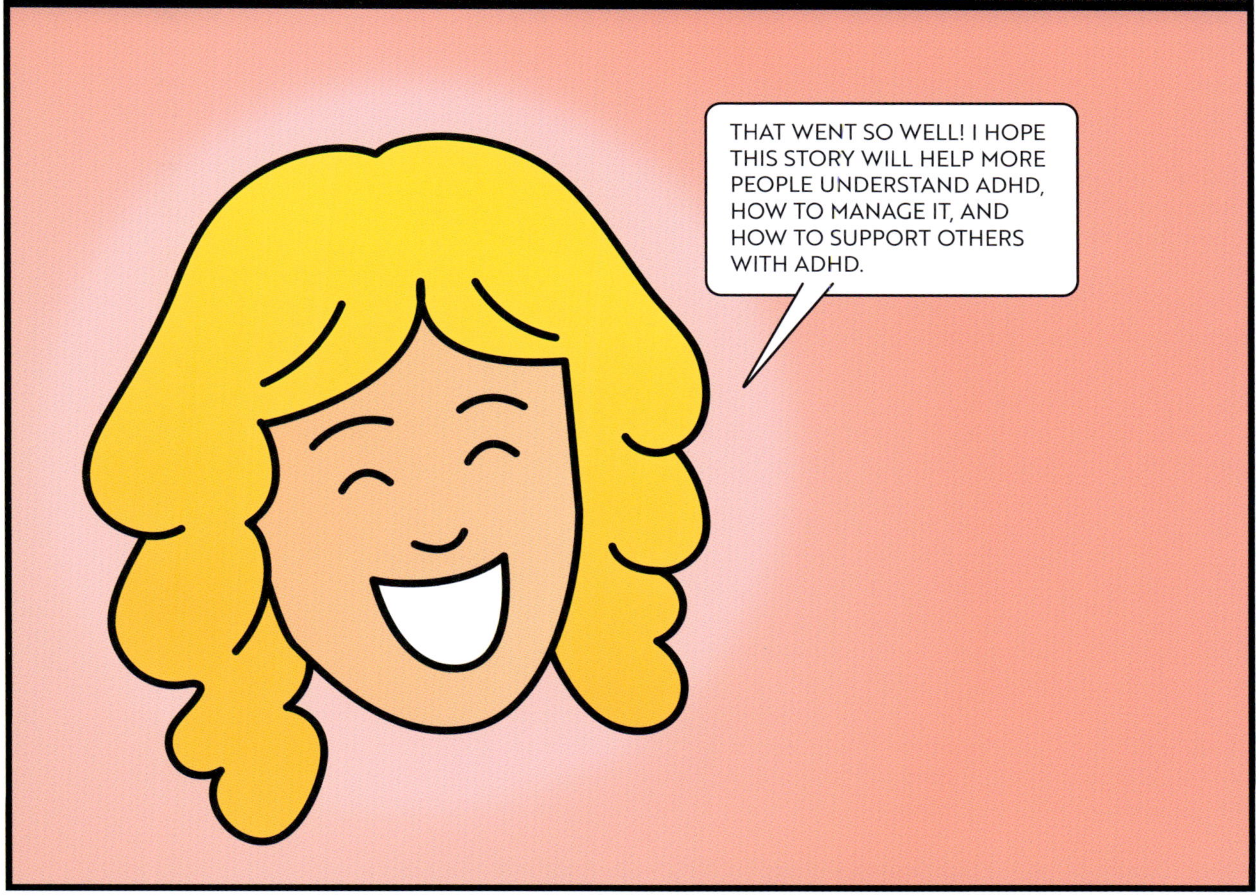
THAT WENT SO WELL! I HOPE THIS STORY WILL HELP MORE PEOPLE UNDERSTAND ADHD, HOW TO MANAGE IT, AND HOW TO SUPPORT OTHERS WITH ADHD.

KEY TERMS

behavior modification plan: plan that involves setting clear expectations, managing or limiting negative behavior triggers, and encouraging and rewarding positive behavior. The plan needs agreement from both a child and parents or caregivers.

executive functioning: mental abilities needed to plan, organize and carry out (execute) tasks. These functions follow four main pathways in the brain and may be altered for someone with ADHD.

genetics: the study of genes — the sections of DNA inside cells that code for many of a person's traits, such as eye color. Genetics looks at the various traits coded in genes, and how they are passed from parents to children.

hyperactive: prone to excessive or restless activity

hyperfocus: ability to focus intensely and for a long time on a task that is particularly interesting

impulsive: acting or speaking too quickly. This may seem to happen without thinking.

inattentive: having difficulty focusing and maintaining attention

learning differences: unique challenges in the way a person learns and thinks, related to skills like writing, reading, math, speech or focus. These difficulties stem from differences in the way the brain is "wired."

neurobehavioral: related to how changes in the brain affect learning, behavior and emotions

nonstimulant medication: prescription medicine used to manage symptoms of ADHD without stimulants to affect neurotransmitters in the brain. This type of medicine may be tried after other options, instead of or in addition to stimulants.

stimulant medication: prescription medicine often used to manage symptoms of ADHD. This type of medicine works by boosting and balancing levels of certain chemicals called neurotransmitters in the brain.

MORE INFORMATION FROM THE MEDICAL EDITOR

By Angela C. Mattke, M.D.
Consultant, Community Pediatric & Adolescent Medicine, Mayo Clinic, Rochester, Minnesota;
Assistant Professor of Pediatrics, Mayo Clinic College of Medicine and Science

Attention-deficit/hyperactivity disorder (ADHD) involves problems with attention, **hyperactivity** and **impulsive** behavior. It is a **neurobehavioral** condition, which means it's related to how the brain affects learning and behavior. ADHD also affects the brain's ability to plan, organize and complete tasks — skills known as **executive functioning**. Symptoms start in childhood and may continue into adulthood. They can make it harder to do well in school and can cause problems with family and friends.

Most kids have a short attention span at some point. This is part of typical development. To diagnose ADHD, a healthcare professional carefully considers how certain behaviors affect the child's relationships and ability to function, both at home and at school.

No single cause of ADHD is known. Many factors may contribute. **Genetics** is a big factor. Your environment also can play a role. But ADHD is not the result of bad parenting, a noisy home environment or too much sugar. A child did nothing to cause ADHD.

A diagnosis of ADHD will fall into one of three categories: **inattentive** type, **hyperactive-impulsive** type or combined type. Boys are more likely to be diagnosed with ADHD and tend to have hyperactive or impulsive behaviors. Girls with ADHD tend to be inattentive, which can be more difficult to diagnose.

With ADHD **inattentive** type, people may have difficulty following through with tasks or following directions, paying attention to details, or staying organized. They may appear to be forgetful and easily distracted. People with this type of ADHD may become easily overwhelmed or avoid tasks that are less interesting to them or that require long-term focus. However, "inattentive" ADHD may be better described as "misdirected attention." A child with ADHD can become **hyperfocused** on a task or activity that is especially interesting and not notice other cues.

A child with ADHD **hyperactive-impulsive** type may seem always on the move. The child may show less impulse control, blurting out words or acting quickly. They also may have emotional reactions that seem larger than expected.

A child with ADHD combined type will exhibit a mixture of those symptoms.

Diagnosing ADHD involves a medical exam and history, and a review of multiple areas of the child's life. Other conditions or learning disorders with similar symptoms are ruled out. Parents and teachers contribute feedback on behaviors observed. In general, symptoms must appear by age 12, happen consistently for at least six months, be worse than usual misbehavior and not match with the child's developmental level.

Managing ADHD often involves a combination of medicine, behavioral therapy, and support at home and at school. A **stimulant** or **nonstimulant** medication may be used. A medical professional helps manage and closely monitor this part of treatment.

Parents, caregivers and teachers can help a child with ADHD in a number of ways. Parents and caregivers can establish routines at home, use organizational systems and engage in quality time. A **behavior modification plan** also can help promote positive behaviors. When giving instructions to a child with ADHD, adults should use eye contact and give clear, simple, direct instructions. For kids who can read, written instructions may be especially helpful. Parents and caregivers also should ensure that the child has regular physical activity. Planning with teachers and the school is another critical step in supporting the child's **learning differences**.

With good medical management and support, children with ADHD can be successful in school, at home and in their relationships.

REFERENCES

Danielson ML, et al. ADHD prevalence among U.S. children and adolescents in 2022: Diagnosis, severity, co-occurring disorders, and treatment. *Journal of Clinical Child & Adolescent Psychology*. 2024. doi:10.1080/15374416.2024.2335625.

Wolraich ML, et al. Subcommittee on children and adolescents with attention-deficit/hyperactive disorder. Clinical Practice Guideline for the Diagnosis, Evaluation, and Treatment of Attention-Deficit/Hyperactivity Disorder in Children and Adolescents. *Pediatrics*. 2019. doi:10.1542/peds.2019-2528.

WEB RESOURCES

**ADHD in Kids (for parents) | Nemours KidsHealth —
https://kidshealth.org/en/parents/adhd.html**
Kidshealth.org provides information, education and advice about children's health, behavior and growth. The website is supported by Nemours Children's Health and includes separate sections for kids, teens, parents and educators.

Does my kid have ADHD? All about Attention Deficit-Hyperactivity Disorder — https://mcpress.mayoclinic.org/parenting/does-my-kid-have-adhd-all-about-attention-deficit-hyperactivity-disorder/
Dr. Angela Mattke talks with a child and adolescent psychiatrist at Mayo Clinic to answer many of the most common questions about ADHD from parents and other adults.

Understood – For learning and thinking differences — http://www.understood.org
The website of the nonprofit group Understood shares ideas for skill development and strategies for people with learning differences, as well as for the friends, family and professionals supporting them.

What Is ADHD? Symptoms, Causes, Subtypes, Tests, Treatments — https://www.additudemag.com/what-is-adhd-symptoms-causes-treatments
ADDitude.com is a website focused on better educating the public about ADHD and other related learning differences. The articles are evidence-based, current and easy to understand.

ABOUT THE MEDICAL EDITOR

**Angela C. Mattke, M.D.
Consultant, Community Pediatric & Adolescent Medicine, Mayo Clinic, Rochester, MN;
Assistant Professor of Pediatrics, Mayo Clinic College of Medicine and Science**

Dr. Mattke is a pediatrician at Mayo Clinic Children's Center in Rochester, Minnesota, and is the medical editor of *Mayo Clinic Guide to Raising a Healthy Child*. Dr. Mattke's areas of expertise include adolescent medicine, media use in children and teens, and general pediatrics. In her daily work, she most enjoys seeing her patients smile and helping families who are struggling with health challenges. Dr. Mattke has a special interest in using social media to connect with patients and families and hosts the podcast Kids Health Matters.

ABOUT THE AUTHORS

Guillaume Federighi, aka **Hey Gee**, is a French and American author and illustrator. He began his career in 1998 in Paris, France. He also spent a few decades exploring the world of street art and graffiti in different European capitals. After moving to New York in 2008, he worked with many companies and brands, developing a reputation in graphic design and illustration for his distinctive style of translating complex ideas into simple and timeless visual stories. He is also the owner and creative director of Hey Gee Studio, a full-service creative agency based in New York City.

Evie is 11 years old and loves animals and math. She also enjoys playing with friends, creating stories, playing basketball, watching hockey and playing with her dog, Gus. She lives in Rochester, Minnesota, with her parents, her brother and her dog. Evie has been learning to manage her ADHD since she was diagnosed in second grade after her parents noticed that focusing on reading, following directions, finishing tasks and especially remote learning were particularly challenging for her. She is also learning to manage dyslexia. Evie and her parents want readers to know she is thriving, striving and living her best life.

ABOUT FONDATION IPSEN BOOKLAB

At the service of the general interest, working toward an equitable society, the Fondation Ipsen BookLab publishes and distributes books free of charge, primarily to schools and associations. Through collaborations between experts, artists, authors and children, our publications, for all ages and in a variety of languages, focus on the education and awareness of issues related to health, disability and rare diseases. Discover our complete catalog online at www.fondation-ipsen.org/books.

ABOUT MAYO CLINIC PRESS

Launched in 2019, Mayo Clinic Press shines a light on the most fascinating stories in medicine and empowers individuals with the knowledge to build healthier, happier lives. From the award-winning *Mayo Clinic Health Letter* to books and media covering the scope of human health and wellness, Mayo Clinic Press publications provide readers with reliable and trusted content by some of the world's leading healthcare professionals. Proceeds benefit important medical research and education at Mayo Clinic. For more information about Mayo Clinic Press, visit MCPress.MayoClinic.org.

ABOUT THE COLLABORATION

The My Life Beyond series was developed in partnership between Fondation Ipsen's BookLab and Mayo Clinic, which has provided world-class medical education for more than 150 years. This collaboration aims to provide trustworthy, impactful resources for understanding childhood diseases and other problems that can affect children's well-being.

The series offers readers a holistic perspective of children's lives with — and beyond — their medical challenges. In creating these books, young people who have been Mayo Clinic patients worked together with author-illustrator Hey Gee, sharing their personal experiences. The resulting fictionalized stories authentically bring to life the patients' emotions and their inspiring responses to challenging circumstances. In addition, Mayo Clinic physicians contributed the latest medical expertise on each topic so that these stories can best help other patients, families and caregivers understand how children perceive and work through their own challenges.

Text: Hey Gee and Evie
Illustrations: Hey Gee

Medical editor: Angela C. Mattke, M.D., Consultant, Community Pediatric & Adolescent Medicine, Mayo Clinic, Rochester, MN; Assistant Professor of Pediatrics, Mayo Clinic College of Medicine and Science, Rochester, MN

Managing editor: Anna Cavallo, Health Education and Content Services/Mayo Clinic Press, Mayo Clinic, Rochester, MN
Project manager: Mary E. Curl, Department of Education, Mayo Clinic, Rochester, MN
Manager of publications: Céline Colombier-Maffre, Fondation Ipsen, Paris, France
President: James A. Levine, M.D., Ph.D., Professor, Fondation Ipsen, Paris, France

MAYO CLINIC PRESS KIDS
200 First St. SW
Rochester, MN 55905
MCPress.MayoClinic.org

© 2025 Mayo Foundation for Medical Education and Research (MFMER)

MAYO, MAYO CLINIC and the Mayo triple-shield logo are marks of Mayo Foundation for Medical Education and Research. Published by Mayo Clinic Press Kids, an imprint of Mayo Clinic Press. All rights reserved. No part of this book may be reproduced, stored in a retrieval system, or transmitted, in any form or by any means, electronic, mechanical, photocopying, recording or otherwise, without the prior written permission of the publisher.

The information in this book is true and complete to the best of our knowledge. This book is intended only as an informative guide for those wishing to learn more about health issues. It is not intended to replace, countermand or conflict with advice given to you by your own physician. The ultimate decision concerning your care should be made between you and your doctor. Information in this book is offered with no guarantees. The author and publisher disclaim all liability in connection with the use of this book.

For bulk sales to employers, member groups and health-related companies, contact Mayo Clinic, 200 First St. SW, Rochester, MN 55905, or send an email to SpecialSalesMayoBooks@mayo.edu.

Proceeds from the sale of every book benefit important medical research and education at Mayo Clinic.

ISBN: 979-8-88770-387-9 (HC); 979-8-88770-388-6 (ePub)

Library of Congress Control Number: 2025002169

Library of Congress Cataloging-in-Publication Data is available upon request.

Printed in the United States of America